GERTRUDE, GUMSHOE:
Murder at Goodwill

ROBIN MERRILL

New Creation Publishing

New Creation Publishing
Madison, Maine

This is a work of fiction. Names, characters, businesses,
organizations, places, events, and incidents are either the products
of the author's imagination or used in a fictitious manner. Any
resemblance to actual persons, living or dead, or actual events is
purely coincidental.

Cover by Taste & See Design
Formatting by PerryElisabethDesign.com

Library of Congress Control Number: 2016918989

ISBN-10: 0-9985198-0-4
ISBN-13: 978-0-9985198-0-7

Acknowledgements:

Thank you a million times over to my first readers: Cari, Tracey, Julie, Laura, Eddie, and of course, Mom. It brings me so much joy to share my beloved characters with you.

More Books by Robin Merrill

GERTRUDE, GUMSHOE

Introducing Gertrude, Gumshoe

CHRISTIAN FICTION

Shelter

Daniel

The Witches of Commack, Maine

Grace Space: A Direct Sales Tale

DEVOTIONALS

The Jesus Diet: How the Holy Spirit Coached Me to a 50-Pound Weight Loss

More Jesus Diet: More of God, Less of Me, Literally

For Josh

A Note from the Author

Please understand: I *love* Goodwill. Most of my wardrobe came from Goodwill. This story is not meant to disparage this wonderful organization, but to pay a sort of homage to it. I am confident that Goodwill has always been and will always be a safe place to shop.

1

Christmas was coming, and Gertrude didn't have all her shopping done yet. Actually, she didn't have *any* of her shopping done yet. But she really only had to shop for her sister Harriet, and she wanted to get something for Isaiah and Elijah, two little boys from her church.

Gertrude didn't usually shop at Goodwill; it was just too pricey for her taste, but they were having a dollar sale that weekend, and she knew Goodwill would have games and toys.

So, she called the CAP bus. CAP stood for Community Action Program, a county-run organization that provided free transportation to people who qualified.

The CAP bus pulled into Gertrude's trailer park fifteen minutes later. Gertrude threw on her coat, said goodbye to her many cats, and headed out into the cold. She was happy to see that Norman was driving. She liked the cut of Norm's jib.

"How are things, Norm?" she said as she hoisted herself into the van.

"Oh you know, the usual."

She banged the snow off the feet of her walker and slid the van door shut. "Ah, nice and toasty in here," she said. She really didn't like being cold. The older she got, the less she liked it.

"I aim to please," Norman said. "Where to?"

"I need to go to Goodwill, do some Christmas shopping."

Norman chuckled, but he didn't argue. He drove his van around the one-way loop that served as Gertrude's street, and then pulled out onto Route 150 in the small Maine town of Mattawooptock. Goodwill was only a few miles away, and it didn't take long to get there, despite the sloppy driving conditions. He pulled the van up to the front door. "Do you know how long you'll be?"

"Yeah, probably a couple of hours," Gertrude said. "I like to make sure I see everything."

Norman shook his head. "Only you could spend a couple of hours in Goodwill. My shift will probably be over by then. But just call for a bus. They'll let you use their phone."

"No need, Norm! I got my own jitterbug now!"

"You do?" Norman asked, shocked.

"Yep!" she proudly declared. "You want my number?"

"Nah, that's OK. I'll get it later. You have fun shopping now."

"Always do!" Gertrude said, and slid out of the van. Then she slipped and slid her way through the slush toward the big, glass double doors.

Goodwill was *packed* on this Saturday morning. Gertrude couldn't believe that so many people could afford to shop at Goodwill. The kids' corner of the store was completely swamped. There were little rugrats everywhere.

Gertrude stowed her walker neatly in the near corner of the store, and replaced it with a shopping cart. Then she headed, with some trepidation, toward the masses.

She wisely avoided the clothing racks, and weaved her way through strollers and shopping carts to the toy section. Here, there were only kids, so Gertrude was the same height as everyone else. She saw a stuffed panda that she thought Elijah might like, but as she reached for it, a grubby toddler grabbed it from beneath her hand. Gertrude gave the girl a dirty look, but resisted the urge to snatch it out of her sticky little paws. She surveyed the remaining toys before her and found a colorful stuffed dinosaur. She snatched it and looked it over. Only one dollar. In pretty good shape. No holes or stains. Only a few stray dog hairs. She could pick those off later. She threw the stuffed dino into her empty cart. Now, for Isaiah. He was a little older, so she wanted to get him a big-boy present. Her eyes traveled to the puzzles. Aha! *But wait, how do I know there are no missing pieces in these puzzles?* In the end, Gertrude decided it was worth the gamble. She had a vast collection of "extra" puzzle pieces at home. If the puzzle she purchased had any holes, she was certain she could find something in her collection of extras that would work. So, after a little ado, she decided on a forty-piece puzzle depicting a tank full of colorful, tropical fish. She thought Isaiah would like it. She was also starting not to care, as she was really getting tired of hanging out in the kids' section. There were just too many kids there.

She tossed the puzzle into her cart. Now, for her sister Harriet. She pushed her cart out of the kids' section and then looked around, wondering where to go next. She didn't want to look at clothes, because a) they were expensive, and b) Harriet was no Slim Pickens. Gertrude didn't want to buy her something that was too small, or, heaven forbid, too big. She'd never hear the end of it.

I know! Perfume! Gertrude knew from past visits that, in another corner of the store, a small section was devoted to things that smelled fancy: cosmetics, soaps, lotions, and such. She pushed her cart out of the fray and toward the perfume section, which appeared to be empty.

As she rounded the corner to come into the perfume aisle, she saw that the section wasn't *entirely* empty, and she let out a little shriek.

There, on the floor, lay a young woman, who, judging from the pool of blood around her tousled, wavy, brunette locks, was very dead. Only inches from the unfortunate woman's head lay the ugliest lamp Gertrude had ever seen. She marveled at how the lamp was fearsome enough to stand out and startle her, despite its proximity to a dead person. The thing was an awful green, a shade straight out of a 1970s kitchen. She had a dishwasher bearing that same tint of avocado tucked away in her trailer. Not only was the lamp this regrettable hue, it also bore a lampshade in a clashing shade of lime. And it got even worse. Suspended from the hideous lampshade were several decorative birds. Though Gertrude was fairly confident that they were not, the birds appeared to be taxidermic. She scooched to try to peer at the birds through the thick layer of dust they each bore, and that's how the hordes found her when they arrived in response to her shriek: crouched over a dead body.

She heard several gasps and looked up to see about a dozen faces looking at her in horror. "I just found her like this!" Gertrude cried.

She scanned the faces and could tell that many didn't believe her. As if she would just decide to thump some strange woman in Goodwill with the world's ugliest dead-bird-lamp. Mothers were shielding children's eyes from the scene, and a man in remarkably thick glasses gruffly told Gertrude to "Get back!"

"I didn't do anything!" Gertrude cried. "I can prove it too! That lamp will not have my fingerprints, and look," she added, holding her hands up, "I'm not wearing gloves!"

"What lamp?" the mean man in thick spectacles asked, looking around.

Gertrude looked down at the blood. *What in tarnation?* Sure enough, the lamp had vanished, though there was a smear in the pool of blood, marking where the lamp had been. Gertrude looked around at the crowd, searching their hands, carts, and bags, but she didn't see the lamp, or any blood. She began searching their faces, but she didn't see anyone who looked particularly guilty.

A woman who looked to be in charge pushed her way through the crowd. "Everyone, please leave this aisle. The police have been called. They'll be here shortly. They've asked me not to let anyone leave the store, but please, let's give this poor woman some space."

At first, Gertrude thought the speaker meant to call her, Gertrude, the "poor woman," but then she realized the speaker had meant the dead one. Gertrude backed out of the aisle, pulling her cart with her, still looking for the lamp.

"Did anyone see or hear anything?" Gertrude asked loudly, but she was summarily ignored. She pushed her cart through the crowd, not bothering with time-consuming niceties, until she had circled around to the other end of the closed-off aisle. She squatted to look at the scene from a different angle, and then she saw it. A dirty, dead bird. Only one. But it had to have belonged to that lamp; there was just no other excuse for its existence. It had rolled, slid, or drifted just under the lip of a bottom shelf, so it was invisible to anyone standing upright. Gertrude tried to be sneaky as she reached under the shelf to retrieve the bird, but she needn't have worried. No one was paying her any mind. She snatched the bird and slid it into the pocket of her plaid jumpsuit.

She was looking around for other clues and birds when she heard a voice she recognized, but wished she didn't. "All of you, go to the area in front of the fitting rooms. Someone will be there shortly to speak with you," Deputy Hale of the Somerset County Sheriff's Department ordered.

People began to obediently file toward the changing rooms. Gertrude stayed put.

"Oh great," Hale said, "you again."

2

"You should be happy to see me," Gertrude said to Hale. "I know what the murder weapon was, and someone here moved it, because it's gone."

"Oh yeah? What was it?" Hale asked without looking at her.

"It was an ugly green lamp with dead birds hanging off it. Well, the birds weren't really dead. At least, I don't think so, but they looked dead. And they were filthy!"

"OK. Thanks for that. Now you can join everyone over by the fitting rooms."

"Aren't you going to write that down?" Gertrude asked. "Don't you want more details about the dead-bird-lamp?"

Hale finally looked at her. They had a short staring contest, and then he said, "No. I got it."

"Well, what about security cameras?"

"This is Goodwill," he said.

"Yeah, and I'm pretty sure people steal from Goodwill!"

"No cameras," Hale said, and pointed at the crowd on the opposite side of the room. "Now go."

Gertrude gave him a dirty look, and then headed that way. *It's too bad he's such a jerk*, she thought on her way there. *'Cause he's really quite handsome. But isn't that the way? Young, good looking, pompous jerk. He'll probably run for mayor.*

Gertrude parked her cart alongside another. She leaned her forearms on her cart's handle and then surveyed the contents of the cart beside her. Apparently, this shopper had trouble saying no. Her cart was overflowing with goodies. Gertrude spotted a hen and rooster salt and pepper shaker set and sneakily moved that to her own cart. No one noticed. They were all too busy craning their necks toward the crime scene.

Gertrude didn't want to let go of the cart, but she forced herself to do so, so that she could move about the crowd, looking for clues. Marveling at the fact that no one was paying her any mind—she might as well have been invisible—she looked closely at people's hands, in their carts, and she was even able to peer into a few purses. Had she not been such a morally upstanding individual, she could have even kiped a few wallets. Of course, she did not.

She did, however, notice that one of the Goodwill employees was acting awfully suspiciously. She eyed him closely. He was sweating profusely, though he was only wearing a T-shirt under his blue apron, and the store didn't exactly have the heat cranked up.

"You all right, fella?" she asked.

He looked at her as if surprised she had noticed his existence. "Um ... yeah? I've just, I've never seen a dead body before," he said.

"I see. Well, you get used to it. This is my second."

He didn't respond.

"What's your name?" Gertrude asked.

"Roderick." He looked down at his nametag as if to make sure he'd gotten it right. Then he looked back at her.

"I'm Gertrude."

He nodded, still looking at her.

Bonus points for eye contact, she thought. "Did you kill her?"

"No!" Roderick cried, loud enough to draw attention from several people nearby. "Why would I kill her? I didn't even know her! I mean, she came in here a lot, and I thought she was pretty, but I didn't know her. I don't know anyone. I just work here."

Gertrude stared at him closely.

"Why are you looking at me like that?" he asked. He sounded terrified.

"I'm trying to see if you're lying or not," Gertrude said.

"Of course I'm not lying! I wouldn't lie. I don't lie! Well, not usually …"

"Everything OK here?" the woman who appeared to be in charge asked. She was also wearing a blue apron. Her nametag said "Manager" and "Sherri." She had short spiky hair, but the spikes were in neat rows, and her makeup was flawless.

"Your hair is very organized," Gertrude observed.

"Thank you," Sherri said without a blink.

"And your makeup looks fancy. Is that Grace Space?"

"No," Sherri said. "Are you all right, Roderick?"

"Yes, Sherri. This lady was just asking me lots of questions. I think she thinks I killed that woman with the pretty hair. But I didn't. I wouldn't kill anyone, would I, Sherri? You know me! You know I wouldn't hurt anyone."

"Yes, Roderick. I know you. And I'm sure that's not what this customer was implying. Isn't that right?" Sherri asked, giving Gertrude a stern look.

"Yes, that's right, Roderick," Gertrude said. "I was just asking if you killed her. I wasn't saying that you did."

"But I didn't!" Roderick cried.

Gertrude eyed him closely. Then, satisfied, she said, "I believe you."

A deputy stepped toward them. "You were the first one to find the body?" he asked Gertrude.

"I was."

"Excuse me for a minute, folks," the deputy said to Sherri and Roderick. He took several steps off to the side, obviously expecting Gertrude to follow. She did, after a momentary delay to retrieve her cart.

"Can you tell me what you saw?" he asked.

She leaned forward on the cart handle and whispered, "I saw the woman lying on the floor—"

"Why are you whispering?" the deputy asked.

Gertrude looked around. She leaned toward him. He leaned away from her. "I'm certain the murderer is still in here," she whispered.

"OK then," the deputy said doubtfully. "Please continue."

"So, she was obviously dead, because there was so much blood. There was also a green lamp lying in the blood. I think that might have been the murder weapon."

The cop looked up. "We didn't find any green lamp."

"I know," Gertrude said, grateful that someone was at least listening to her about the stupid lamp. "When I looked up, it disappeared."

"And you didn't see anyone take it?"

"No. If I had, I would have mentioned that by now. It was there, and then someone snatched it out of the blood. Probably the murderer. If you find that green lamp, you'll find the murderer. The lamp was really ugly, and dirty, and it had dead birds hanging off it."

"OK then. Did you see or hear anything else?"

"You don't believe me," Gertrude observed.

"I didn't say that."

"I can tell by the way you're looking at me. You think I'm bonkers."

"Ma'am, I've got a lot of people I've got to talk to. Did you see anything else?"

"Don't call me ma'am," Gertrude said.

He took that as a no, and moved on to question Roderick. Gertrude followed, but was stealthy about it.

"Do you mind if I sit in on this?" Sherri asked. "I'm the manager, and Roderick struggles with anxiety."

I'll say, Gertrude thought.

"That would be fine," the deputy said to Sherri. "So," he said to Roderick, "can you tell me what happened?"

"Sure," Roderick said. "I heard a lady scream"—

I didn't scream, Gertrude thought defensively, *I just gasped. Maybe a little yelp. But not a scream! I'm a professional, for crying out loud.*

—"so I went to the soap section, and I saw another lady lying on the floor. I thought she was dead, so I went to get Sherri. And she called the police. Then me and her went back to the soap section. Then you got here. And you told us to come stand—"

"OK," the deputy interrupted. "Did you hear or see anything else, in or near the soap section, maybe before you heard the scream?"

I didn't scream!

"No," Roderick said quickly. Too quickly.

The policeman looked suspicious. "Have you seen anyone in here tonight, anyone behaving unusually or suspiciously?"

Gertrude stifled a laugh. *Only everyone?*

Roderick just shook his head.

"And did you know the woman?" the policeman asked.

"The dead one?"

The deputy nodded.

"No. She came in here to shop a lot. But I didn't know her. I mean, I've seen her. A lot. But I don't know her. I don't even know her name."

"OK then. Thank you," the deputy said. Then he turned to Sherri. "Let's step over this way," he said, and took her far enough away so that Gertrude couldn't hear what they were saying.

She sidled up to Roderick. "So, how hard is it to get a job here?"

"I dunno," Roderick said.

"Well, how did you get a job here?"

"I dunno," Roderick said, and walked away.

How rude, Gertrude thought.

3

Gertrude sat in her recliner, eating pickles straight out of the jar, thinking about the events of the day. She had decided to take the case. No, probably no one would pay her, but if she could get another win under her belt, perhaps people who did need to hire an investigator would take her more seriously.

And once again, she knew more about the case than the police did, simply because the police wouldn't listen to her. She had dusted her secret bird off and placed him on a TV tray beside her recliner. And Fog, one of the newest additions to her feline family, had promptly swatted it to the floor. But she had rescued it from further deadness, and now she held it in her hand and stared at it as she crunched on her pickle.

The bird seemed to be made of wood, with fake feathers and eyeballs glued on. It was hideous. Even more so since she had dusted it off. But despite its lack of aesthetic appeal, it could be the key to finding Tislene's murderer.

Gertrude had learned from the news that the victim was Tislene Breen, a twenty-five-year-old Mattawooptock local. According to Channel 5, Tislene was unemployed, unmarried, and had no children. Hence, Gertrude wasn't sure where to start with her investigation.

She knew that she could look Tislene up on the Internet and probably find some information. But the library was already closed for the day. She could go visit her neighbor, Old Man Crow; he had a computer. But he was also a cranky old coot, and she didn't want to deal with him.

Wait! she thought suddenly. *I'm not paying this whopping cellular telephone bill for nothing!* She fished her phone out of her walker pouch, and—though she took a circuitous route—made her way to Facebook and located Tislene Breen's profile. Lucky for Gertrude's investigation, Tislene didn't care much about privacy settings.

Apparently Tislene had lots of friends, more than a thousand, according to the social media behemoth. This number was supported by the fact that her profile page was chock-full of sad goodbyes. Gertrude read through them all painstakingly, learning essentially nothing, and eventually got to the stuff Tislene had posted before she died. She scoured these posts and photos for any hint of a conflict, but she found none. There were only pictures of Tislene laughing with friends; Tislene drinking beer; Tislene posing in the front seat of a car; Tislene posing in the backseat of a car; Tislene posing on a snowmobile. From what Gertrude could tell, Tislene had been a fun-loving, carefree girl, who loved to take pictures of herself. If she had enemies, there was no evidence of them on Facebook.

Either everyone's life was *much* better than Gertrude's, or no one told the truth on Facebook. Gertrude knew she had to actually talk to a real person. But who?

Gertrude clicked on a face claiming to be Tislene's sister. *Maybe I could send her a message through Facebook. Ask her a few questions that way.* She pressed the message icon. Then she noticed a cute little phone icon. *I can call her through Facebook?* She pressed the blue phone.

"Hello?"

"Hello. This is Gertrude. Are you Tislene's sister?"

Significant pause. "Who is this?"

"Gertrude."

"Yeah, you said that. But I don't know any Gertrude."

"Well, I'm Gertrude, and I'm investigating your sister's murder."

"Oh, are you a cop?"

Gertrude scrunched up her nose. "No, but I'm an investigator. Can I ask you a few questions?"

"You know it's like ten o'clock?"

Gertrude pulled her phone away from her ear to look at the time. Then she put the phone back to her ear. "Yes. I see that now."

"Well, do you always do your investigating this late?"

"Who do you think killed your sister?"

"Wow. Getting right to the point, aren't you?"

Gertrude didn't say anything. She just waited.

"Like I told the cops, I have no idea who killed Tislene. She didn't have any enemies. She didn't do drugs, except for pot. She's never stolen anyone's husband or boyfriend, at least not since high school—"

"She stole someone's husband in high school?" Gertrude interjected, mortified.

"No! I mean high school is like the Wild West of hormones. We were all fighting. But that was a long time ago. I'm pretty sure no one from high school decided to kill my sister in Goodwill. I mean, it doesn't sound like something that was well-planned, right? It sounds like some nutjob decided to hit my sister in the head. I doubt her killer even knew who she was."

Gertrude nodded, thinking.

"Are we done?"

"I suppose so," Gertrude said. "Can I give you my number in case you think of anything else?"

"I guess."

"OK. You got a pen?" Gertrude asked.

"Yep."

"It sounds like you're lying."

"What?"

"Do you really have a pen?"

"Yes! Just give me the stupid number!"

"OK. 5 ..."

"Yeah?"

"Did you get the 5?"

"Yes!"

Gertrude couldn't imagine why the woman sounded so exasperated, but chalked her rudeness up to grief. She gave her the rest of the phone number and then hung up. Then she thought better of it, and called back.

"What?!"

"Can you think of anyone else I could call? Maybe someone who knew Tislene better than you?"

"I'm her sister. No one knows, I mean *knew*, Tizzy better than I did."

"Well, there's no way her life was perfect," Gertrude remarked.

"I didn't say her life was perfect. I said she had no enemies. She was easygoing. She just wanted to have fun, but she was poor as dirt and never really found a job she liked. She wasn't exactly a genius and wasn't a big success or anything, but that doesn't mean she deserved to be murdered in a thrift store!"

"All right then. Can you think of anyone else I should call?"

"No!" The grieving sister hung up.

Gertrude decided it might be more fruitful to focus on finding the murder weapon. She wouldn't need to figure out motive if she had fingerprints. But, just where was that stupid lamp? She had to get back into Goodwill. The lamp could be, probably was, long gone by now, but she had to make sure. Maybe it was simply stashed in a pile of mismatched linens. Who knew?

Vowing to revisit Goodwill in the morning, Gertrude decided it was way past her bedtime. She checked to make sure her door was locked. (She'd been doing so every night since a stripper had snuck in in the middle of the night and knocked over her slinkies.) Then she changed into some footed pajamas, washed her face, brushed her teeth, and climbed into bed. Some of the cats on her bed jumped out of the way to make a hole for her, but as soon as Gertrude was settled in, they returned, so that almost every part of Gertrude's body was touching a cat. In this comfy, cozy way, Gertrude drifted off to sleep, and dreamed about dead, dusty birds.

In the morning, Gertrude practically bounced out of bed, hurriedly got ready, and then called the CAP bus. Then she waited impatiently by her door, peering out the window, and wishing she hadn't donned the coat and hat just yet.

Finally, the CAP bus pulled alongside her trailer, and she said goodbye to the cats and left.

"Where to, Gertrude?" Norman asked.

"Back to Goodwill."

"Again? I would think you would be a little freaked out, after everything that happened there yesterday. You were still there, weren't you, when they found the body?"

"Not only was I there, *I'm* the one who found her. And now I'm going back to find the murder weapon."

Norman groaned. "Not again. Gertrude, you need to give it up. You're not a detective. You're not even a cop. You're just going to get yourself hurt—or worse."

"Thanks for your concern, Norm. But I'll be fine. I pinky swear it." She stuck out a crooked little pinky finger toward Norman. He glanced at the pinky out of the corner of his eye, but chose to ignore it.

Norman pulled into the Goodwill parking lot, which was already packed, though the store had just opened. "Lots of rubbernecks, looks like," Norman said.

Gertrude paused with her hand on the door handle. "Well, this just gets my goat. How am I supposed to find any evidence with all those civilians contaminating my crime scene?"

Norman chuckled. "Civilians? Gertrude, *you're* a civilian, and I'm pretty sure the 'crime scene' has already been processed, or the sheriff wouldn't have let the store open."

Gertrude opened the door. "Fine then. I guess I have to do more than just shop here," she said, climbing out.

As she pulled her walker out after her, Norman asked, "What's that mean?"

"It means I need to get a job," Gertrude said, and slid the van door shut. Then she turned and walked into the store.

As the door closed behind her, she surveyed the scene before her. Had she not known any differently, she wouldn't have imagined that someone had been murdered there the day before. It looked like an ordinary, albeit crowded, Goodwill. Although, she did notice, there were more people than usual in the perfume section.

She approached the customer service desk, where Sherri was ringing customers up.

"Excuse me," Gertrude interrupted.

Sherri didn't even look up. "I'll be right with you," she said.

Gertrude sighed and leaned on her walker to wait. She saw Roderick peek around a corner and then, when he saw her see him, he ducked back behind the shelves.

Good grief that man is peculiar, Gertrude thought.

"How can I help you?" Sherri asked.

Gertrude appeared to have Sherri's undivided attention. "I would like to work here."

"OK, great," Sherri said, her face deadpan. "You can apply online."

"Oh," Gertrude said. "Well, can't I apply right now? I'm already here."

"Sorry. We only accept online applications."

"I don't have Internet at my house," Gertrude said.

"You can access the Internet for free at the public library," Sherri said, as if she'd said that a hundred times before.

"Or!" Gertrude exclaimed. "Can't I just use my jitterbug?" She pulled out her Android.

"I suppose so," Sherri said, and turned to ring up the next customer in line.

Gertrude stabbed at the browser icon and then navigated her way to Goodwill's website. Before long, she was trying not to cuss as her chubby, stubby fingers tried to type her info into those tiny fields.

Twenty minutes later, she had officially applied for a job and had a significant crick in her neck. She stretched, rubbed her neck, and looked around, wondering what to do next.

She decided she might as well do some snooping. So she traded her walker in for a shopping cart and tried to act nonchalantly as she made her way toward the swinging doors marked "Employees Only." Anytime an employee neared or passed through the doors, Gertrude would pause and feign interest in whatever was closest, which at one point was a bag of golf clubs.

She had finally arrived at the doors, and was about to push her cart through them, when someone busted out through them like a gunslinger storming a saloon. The cart protected Gertrude from injury, but she was knocked off balance, and the doors hitting the cart made a terrific crash.

"What are you doing?" the man with thick glasses cried.

Gertrude steadied herself on the cart handle with one hand and checked her hair with the other. "Why, I could ask you the same thing!" she cried. She wasn't sure if that made any sense, but she was still a bit shaken by the collision.

The man looked confused. Gertrude often had this effect on people. He pointed at the door and spoke very slowly, "Employees only. You can't go back there."

"What's your name?" Gertrude asked.

The man scowled. Then he pointed at his own nametag and slowly said, "Matt," giving the "t" sound far more emphasis than necessary.

"Hi, Matt. I'm Gertrude. Did you kill Tislene Breen?"

"What? Of course not. Do I need to get the manager? Because she won't put up with this kind of crap."

"Why would you call the manager? I just asked you a question," Gertrude tried.

"Are you going to stay out of the employee only area?"

Good grief. This man isn't even making sense. "Yes, Matt. I will stay out of the employee only area." Gertrude tried to quickly spin away and stalk off with attitude, a move she had perfected with her walker, but it was quite clumsy with the shopping cart and she ended up doing a cumbersome five-point turn instead. Any sassy effect was lost. By the time she headed down the dishes aisle, Matt was out of sight, and Gertrude turned around again—only a three-point-turn this time—and pushed through the swinging doors. This time she made it through, and as the doors swung closed behind her, she paused to take in the scene, and wondered where to look first. There were bins everywhere. Bins of clothes, bins of books, bins of shoes, bins of dishes. *This is what heaven must look like*, Gertrude thought, and started toward the closest bin.

She didn't get there.

"You need to leave. Right now." A sharp voice spoke from behind. Gertrude looked over her shoulder and found Sherri, the manager with the organized hair.

"I was just looking for the bathroom," Gertrude lied.

Sherri's facial expression made it perfectly clear she knew this was a lie, but she said, "No problem. I'd be happy to show you. Right this way."

Feeling beaten, Gertrude walked by Sherri as she held the door open for her. Then she followed Sherri to the bathroom. Gertrude smiled, said, "Thank you," and then entered the bathroom and locked the door behind her. She leaned on the sink and looked at herself in the mirror. She counted to sixty.

When she figured she'd waited long enough, she discreetly poked her head out of the bathroom and looked around. No Sherri. No Matt. She slipped through the doorway and returned to her cart. Then, she slinked her way to the linens. She felt through every pile. No lumps. She went to housewares to look at the actual lamps. No dead birds. She opened every drawer in every desk and every dresser. Nothing. She surreptitiously began to look for trash cans. This took her back into the restroom, but no lamps in that trash can. She looked around and then furtively ducked into the men's room, but that trash can was also disappointing. The only trash cans left in the store were those small ones beside each register. She headed that way.

Sherri looked at her suspiciously, and Gertrude feigned interest in the odd assortment of items in the locked glass case: a knife; jewelry; some fine china (three teacups and four saucers); and what may or may not have been an actual Coach purse.

As Sherri got busy checking out customers, Gertrude was able to verify that there was no ugly green lamp in any of the trash cans.

She traded her shopping cart in for her walker and then headed outside to the dumpster.

It was nearly empty, except for one garbage bag. She picked up a nearby stick and jabbed at the bag until it ripped open. It was full of mostly food waste, including something that looked like pink noodles, and Gertrude spread it around the bottom of the dumpster until she was confident there was no green lamp hiding among the chicken bones. She dropped the stick and started to walk off. But then she couldn't help herself. She went back to the dumpster and reached into it to try to retrieve a plastic Folgers coffee container. She used these to sort some of her smaller collections, and one just can't have too many. Her fingers just brushed the top of the red coffee container, but she couldn't quite get a grip.

She was thinking about how to climb into the dumpster when she heard a vehicle pull up behind her. She looked up.

Hale climbed out of his cruiser. "You again," he said to her. "You know, dumpster diving is illegal."

"No it's not. Why are you always trying to scare me with make-believe laws?"

4

On Tuesday morning, Sherri called Gertrude and invited her to come in for an interview.

Gertrude was ecstatic. She'd never had an interview before.

She changed three times before deciding on an outfit. She finally settled on a knee-length dress with a floral pattern that was mostly orange. In truth, she wasn't sure if it was a dress or a housecoat, but when she put it on over red tights, she looked absolutely smashing. She added a string of chunky yellow beads for further flare.

She felt quite confident as she pushed her walker through the Goodwill doors. She didn't see Sherri anywhere, but she did see Matt running a register. She approached him warily.

"Excuse me."

"What?" Matt snapped before he'd even looked at her. She didn't answer, so he did look up at her and then became evidently disgusted. "Now what do you want?"

"I'm here for a job interview."

"You're joking."

"I am not," Gertrude said indignantly.

Matt rolled his eyes, but he did grab a radio from beside his register and spoke into it. "Sherri, the crazy lady from yesterday is here for a job interview."

"I'll be right there," came a terse reply.

True to her word, Sherri materialized within seconds, and, without so much as a glance toward Gertrude, marched right up to Matt, leaned on the counter and spoke quietly, but sternly, to him. Gertrude strained to hear, but she couldn't. Still, the red creeping up Matt's neck led Gertrude to believe he was being scolded.

Gertrude saw Matt nod, and then Sherri turned her attention to Gertrude. "Can I help you?"

"Yes. I'm here for a job interview."

"And your name is?"

"Gertrude."

Sherri looked at her watch. "You're an hour early."

"Early bird gets the worm."

Sherri looked at her, incredulous.

Gertrude shrugged and tried to smile.

"All right then," Sherri said. "Follow me."

Sherri led her to the back of the store, and Gertrude became excited when she realized Sherri was leading her to the big employee only swinging double doors—the gates of paradise. Sherri held one open and ushered Gertrude through. Then Sherri led her to a small, crooked desk in the corner of the room. "Have a seat," she said, motioning to a metal folding chair. With a little effort, Gertrude sat. Sherri sat down on the other side of the desk. "So," she began, and cleared her throat, "I didn't realize when reviewing your application that you were you."

Gertrude scowled.

"What I mean is," Sherri corrected herself, "I didn't know, by looking at your name, that you were the one who found that poor woman's body, and that you were the one wandering around back here yesterday."

"But I applied for the job right in front of you. Do you really receive that many job applications?"

"Well, yes, as a matter of fact. Since the killing, interest in working here has certainly spiked. Which is why I need to ask you ..." Sherri placed her forearms on the desk and leaned forward, leveling a serious gaze at Gertrude. Gertrude had an urge to laugh, but she bit it back. "I'm concerned that your interest in working here might have something to do with the murder."

Was that a question? Am I supposed to say something? Unsure of what to do, she did nothing. She just sat there, expressionless, staring at Sherri and desperately wishing there were a few cats on her lap.

"In other words," Sherri tried again, "do you have some sort of dark fascination with this place because of the crime that was committed here?"

"No," Gertrude said.

Sherri stared at her, as if waiting for her to say more.

Gertrude didn't know what else there was to say.

"OK, so why don't you tell me why you *do* want to work here?"

Gertrude felt her heart rate increase. *I'd better not tell her I'm a gumshoe.* "I like stuff," Gertrude blurted out.

Sherri raised one perfectly groomed and penciled eyebrow. Gertrude marveled at just how high that eyebrow could go, and what a sharp angle it formed at its apex. "You like stuff?" Sherri asked.

"Yes. I find it fascinating. I think I would do a good job here, because I'm good at stuff." She paused. "I'm good *with* stuff," she corrected.

Sherri leaned back in her chair. "All right then. Let's give it a shot. You'll have to go to the hospital and have a drug test performed. Ask the hospital to fax me the results. And we'll have to run a background check on you."

"Really?" Gertrude exclaimed. "That's it?"

Sherri chuckled. "Well, I might have some misgivings, but your references spoke quite highly of you. And I'm a big fan of your pastor, so if he says you're a good risk, then I take him at his word."

Gertrude practically bounced out of Goodwill, flashing a disturbingly triumphant smile at Matt as she passed.

He looked as if he was going to be sick.

5

"I need to go to the hospital," Gertrude told Norman.

"Are you all right?" he asked.

She was surprised, and a little touched, by his concern. She knew he drove people to the hospital all the time.

"Yes. I'm fine. Fit as a fiddle. I just need to go get a drug test for my job."

"Wow! They actually gave you a job?"

"Of course they did! Why wouldn't they? I'm quite a catch!"

"Sorry, didn't mean anything by it. I'm just impressed. Congratulations."

An exceptionally friendly woman named Lizz registered Gertrude at Mattawooptock General. Lizz seemed to think a drug test would be a grand time.

"What are they going to test me for?" Gertrude asked as Lizz led her down a sparkling clean hallway.

"Oh, they just do a general panel of recreational drugs."

"Like what?"

Lizz smiled and pushed an elevator button. "I'm not sure. If you don't take illegal drugs, then you have nothing to worry about."

Gertrude thought for a minute. "Are they going to test me for the grass?"

Lizz laughed. "Yes. Probably. Why, do you smoke marijuana? You don't look the type."

"No. But I've thought about it before. I know how much my cats love their catnip."

Lizz was still laughing. "I don't think it's the same thing."

Lizz left Gertrude with a nurse whose nametag read, "Bessie." Bessie, who was decidedly less friendly than Lizz, led Gertrude into a bathroom, and gave her a small plastic cup.

"What are you testing for?" Gertrude asked.

Bessie rattled off, "Marijuana, opiates, cocaine, phencyclidine, and amphetamines."

Gertrude's eyes grew wide. "What? Don't they make drugs I can pronounce?"

"Just pee in the cup. Then put it in here when you're done." The nurse opened a small cupboard in the bathroom wall.

"What's a fen-say-kli-dee?" Gertrude tried.

The nurse rolled her eyes. "It's a drug we're testing for. Now do your thing." She closed the door, leaving Gertrude alone in the spacious restroom.

"How rude!" Gertrude said aloud to no one. She opened the cabinet door and looked inside. It was empty. *Why am I putting my pee in a cupboard?*

Yet, she did her business and then put the evidence in the small cupboard. She closed the door and then listened for activity inside the cupboard. She soon heard the other side slide open. She ripped open the cupboard door, stuck her head in, and said, "Peekaboo!"

Gertrude couldn't see a face, but the person whose gloved hand was now on her cup gave a frightened gasp.

"Sorry!" Gertrude said. "Didn't mean to scare you. Just thought this fancy cupboard was neat."

The person on the other side did not respond, just slammed the door shut. It was just an empty cupboard again.

Gertrude was back in the comfort of her cat-filled home only minutes later.

She made herself a sandwich and settled in to watch some *Antiques Roadshow*, which was one of her favorite shows. But mostly, she was just waiting for Sherri to call. The minutes dragged by, and Gertrude couldn't help but feel she was losing precious time—she knew, from watching television, that it doesn't take long for a trail to go cold.

She decided she should go visit her neighbor Calvin.

She put herself together, wrapped herself up in warm clothes, and headed out into winter. She carefully made her way over the ice and snow—*only December and already treacherous*—and was soon pounding on Calvin's door with a mittened fist.

"What?" she heard Calvin snap from inside.

"Let me in, Old Man Crow!" Gertrude hollered.

"No!" Calvin hollered back.

She tried the door handle. It turned. She let herself in.

Calvin slammed his recliner into the upright position. "Well, shut the door! You're letting all my heat out. I pay for that, you know!"

She began to take her hat off.

"Don't undress. You're not staying long. What do you want?"

"Well, I wasn't planning to *undress*, Calvin. And what I want is for you to call Frank."

Calvin turned his attention back to the television. "Frank the cop?" he asked.

"The one and only."

"Well, Frank the cop resigned in a cloud of shame and moved to Massachusetts."

"Are you serious?" Gertrude couldn't believe it.

"I am. But, even if he lived in this actual house, I would not talk to him for you. What do you want with Frank? Haven't you done him enough damage?"

"Damage? I saved him from a serial killer!"

Calvin guffawed, but still didn't look away from the TV. "Serial killer? She wasn't a serial killer! She was his girlfriend, and you had her thrown into prison! Now, you can go. It's my nap time."

"Aren't you curious what I want with him?" Gertrude asked.

"Not at all."

"I want to know what the cops have for evidence," she told him anyway.

"Don't care."

"I've got a new case," she said, trying to entice him.

"Not interested."

"Fine, you grump," she muttered, turning to go.

"Can you lock that door on your way out?"

Gertrude most certainly did not.

6

Gertrude passed her drug test, and Sherri called to let her know she could start her training on Thursday morning. Again, Gertrude agonized over what to wear, but ended up going with a yellow dress with large black polka dots over blue leggings. She thought that would work well with her new blue apron.

She wasn't entirely wrong. She did look somewhat coordinated, if not outdated, but the ensemble wasn't exactly slimming.

Sherri tied the apron behind Gertrude's back—without much string to spare—and then came around to the front of her to look her up and down. She nodded and said, "You look great," unconvincingly. Then she motioned for another woman to join them.

"This is Willow," she said to Gertrude. "She is going to train you." Willow was tall, thin, and expressionless.

"Nice to meet—" Gertrude tried.

"Come with me," Willow said tonelessly and turned away from them.

Gertrude looked at Sherri, who said, "Good luck," and headed in the opposite direction.

Gertrude and her walker followed Willow's tight ponytail through the beautiful swinging doors and into the open area in the back. "You'll start out with sorting," Willow said without looking at Gertrude. "People drop their junk off out there," she pointed toward the door, "and then we examine, categorize, and price."

"All right," Gertrude said.

Willow looked at her. "Don't you think you should be writing this down?"

Gertrude shook her head. "Look at, put in piles, put a number on it. Got it."

Willow rolled her eyes. "OK, so let's start with this bin." She pulled a bin closer to them. "Don't touch anything," she said, and disappeared. Gertrude gazed longingly into the bin, but everything was bagged up in black garbage bags, so she couldn't tell what she was looking at. She could feel her heart rate increase. She couldn't believe she'd never thought about working at Goodwill before.

Willow returned and handed Gertrude a pair of rubber gloves.

Gertrude took them and slid them on.

"We always wear gloves," Willow said. "Some of this stuff is completely disgusting. I learned that the hard way."

"But some of it is treasure!" Gertrude offered. She smiled, but then Willow gave her a chilling look, and Gertrude's smile faded. "They don't let you work with the customers, do they?"

Willow glared at her. "Of course they do. I'm the smartest person here. I can't believe Sherri has me wasting my time training you. A monkey could do this job." She snapped her rubber gloves into place and then said, "So let's get this over with."

She tore into one of the trash bags. Gertrude's heart leapt as a variety of brightly colored trinkets spilled out.

"Do we get first dibs on this stuff?" Gertrude asked, breathless.

Willow glowered at her, and then returned her attention to the bin. "Of course not."

"Well, do we get an employee discount?"

Willow didn't look at her this time, but Gertrude knew she was still glowering. "No."

"Well," Gertrude was exasperated, "what *do* we get?"

"Paid."

"I know that," Gertrude snapped. "I mean, don't we get some benefits with the … with the … with the … *stuff?*"

"No." Willow held up a cracked glass bell. "See how this is broken?"

"I'm not blind," Gertrude said.

"So we don't put this out." Willow efficiently overhanded it into a giant box twenty feet away. It smashed on impact.

"What's that?" Gertrude asked, gazing at the box.

"Read the label. Glass recyclables. We recycle almost anything we don't sell. All you have to do is read. You can read, right?"

Gertrude noticed that all the boxes along the far wall were labeled for recycling: glass, miscellaneous electronics, computers, paper and cardboard, clothing. "Wow, you throw all that *away*?" Gertrude asked, wondering if she might be able to paw through it first.

"No. We *recycle* it," Willow said, handing her a stack of books. "Go put those in the book bin over there," she said, pointing with her chin.

"You didn't go over these very good," Gertrude said.

"*Well*," Willow corrected. "And no, we put out almost all the books we receive, unless they're wet or moldy."

"Moldy books?" Gertrude asked, appalled.

"You haven't seen anything yet. I think some people just *try* to gross us out. Go put the books in the bin."

Gertrude did as she was told, though it wasn't easy balancing all the books atop her walker. "Can you just give me one or two books at a time next time?" she asked on her return.

Willow rolled her eyes again. "Why don't I just let you take over?" she said, stepping back from the bin. "I'll just supervise." She folded her arms across her chest.

Gertrude thought this was a great idea. She grabbed two more books and headed over to the book bin. Then she returned and grabbed two more books and headed for the book bin again.

"Oh for crying out loud, you are slower than death. I'll do the books. You do the rest."

"Fine by me," Gertrude said. "I don't really like books."

"Why am I not surprised?" Willow mumbled.

Gertrude picked up a pretty glass frog. It looked like a bookend, but there was only one. "What do I do with this?"

Willow pointed to a bin to their right. "We have a whole section of décor. Go put it in that bin, along with anything else of its kind."

Gertrude did as she was told. Then she returned to the unsorted bin. Willow had already given up on supervising and was back to helping. She began tossing clothing into a nearby bin.

Gertrude held up a small jacket. "What do we do with kids' clothing?"

"All clothing goes in the same bin. We sort it later."

"That doesn't make sense," Gertrude said.

"Then you should talk to management. I'm sure they'd love to hear your input."

"All right. I will." Gertrude too, began tossing clothes into the clothing bin. It was kind of fun. She felt quite mischievous, as if she was getting away with something, throwing other people's belongings about.

"You have to *look* at them first," Willow interrupted her fun.

"Oh, sorry," Gertrude said. She held up a sweater for inspection, and then headed toward the recycled clothing bin.

"What are you doing?" Willow snapped.

"It has a hole in it," Gertrude explained without turning around.

"Get back here!"

Gertrude turned around and trudged back to her trainer, suddenly feeling quite tired after her first half-hour of employment. "What?"

"Let me see."

Gertrude held the sweater up. "See?"

"Yeah, I see. But that's OK. We can sell that. We only recycle clothing that's been completely destroyed."

"Oh." Gertrude reached in for more clothing and went through the pieces one by one, holding them up, pretending to inspect them, and then chucking them into the clothing bin. She didn't exactly know what Willow had meant by "completely destroyed," but she wasn't sure she wanted to know.

Gertrude ripped into another trash bag and a bunch of puzzles spilled out. "What do I do with these?" she asked.

"All games and puzzles go in the toys bin," Willow said, nodding toward another bin.

"Some of these are open. Do we count the pieces first? Make sure they're all there?"

"Don't be stupid," Willow said. "People mix up pieces among puzzles all the time. Counting wouldn't do any good. We'd have to put them together, which we obviously don't have time to do. Now, hurry up. We have more to do."

I hate her, Gertrude decided, and then heard her pastor's voice in her head. *OK fine. But I really don't like her.*

By the time Gertrude had deposited all the puzzles in the toy bin, Willow had finished sorting everything else.

"Now what?" Gertrude asked.

"Now we sort another bin."

"Can we do something else? I think I understand how to sort." Gertrude found it highly unlikely she would find the dead-bird-lamp in a bin of new donations.

"OK, let's go sort the clothes."

Gertrude groaned, but she followed Willow to the clothing bin.

Willow grabbed a giant can of something and began spraying the clothing.

"What in tarnation is that?" Gertrude asked.

"Bug dope."

"Ew!"

"Yep," Willow said as she finished spraying. "You can get everything at Goodwill, except parasites." Willow put the can down and moved to another clothing bin.

Gertrude stood rooted to her spot.

"It's OK," Willow said. "These have already been sprayed. We have to let them sit for a while after spraying."

"All right," Gertrude said, reluctantly approaching the new bin.

She was slow getting started, but soon she got the hang of it. Willow showed her how to use a tagging gun, and Gertrude thought that was great fun. She and Willow sorted and priced clothing until lunchtime. By then, Gertrude was starving. She gratefully followed Willow into the employee break room and collapsed into a chair. She pulled a warm cheese and pickles sandwich out of her walker pouch.

"You can use the fridge if you want," the young woman seated across from her said. Her eyes were so wide they made her face look even rounder than it was. "Sherri is really nice and lets us use the fridge and the microwave."

"Thanks," Gertrude said. "How old are you?" she asked. The girl looked too young to be working there.

"I'm twenty-one," she said proudly. "My name is Azalea. I work here."

"Gertrude," Gertrude said through a mouthful of sandwich. She swallowed. "I work here too."

"You will love to work here. It's the best place ever. Sherri is so smart and so nice and so pretty. You will love it. I love it. It's the best job ever."

"Good," Gertrude responded. "I hope so. How long have you worked here?" Gertrude didn't really care, but she figured Azalea was a suspect and so she should gather information.

"Three years," Azalea said proudly. "It is the first job I've ever had. I love it."

Gertrude nodded. "You mentioned that. Did you know the dead woman?"

Azalea's eyes grew wide and filled with tears. Her bottom lip shook for a second, and then she got up and ran out of the room.

"What did you say?" Willow asked, but she didn't sound accusing.

"I just asked her about the dead woman."

"Oh. Of course. Well, don't mind Azalea. She's not very bright. Loves Goodwill more than any rational person should. She's probably more upset that it happened here than that the woman's dead."

"What about you?" Gertrude asked. "Did you know the victim?"

"No. Seen her around. Why, did you?"

Gertrude shook her head. "How long is lunch?"

"Thirty."

"Thirty what?" Gertrude asked.

"Hours. What do you think? Thirty minutes. We have till 12:30."

Gertrude glanced at the clock. It was already ten past. She hurriedly finished her sandwich so she could go look for the lamp. When she got up, Willow asked, "Where you going in such a hurry?"

"Oh," Gertrude said, frantically trying to think up a lie, "I'm just going to go read the labels on all the recycling boxes."

7

When Gertrude reentered the large back room, she found Roderick holding several bras.

"I'm just going to hang these out," he stammered, answering a question she hadn't asked.

"All right," Gertrude said, because she didn't know what else to say. Then, grateful for the empty room, she darted to the nearest bin and began digging. Nothing. She dug through the next. She found a shiny pizza cutter she desperately wanted, but resisted the urge to steal it. Other than that, nothing. She had pawed through every bin but one when Willow returned. Gertrude, out of breath, tried to look nonchalant, but she could feel that last bin calling to her.

"What have you been doing?" Willow asked. "You're all red!"

"Hot flash," Gertrude lied.

"OK, well, let's start pricing then."

Gertrude groaned, but followed her, and for the next several hours, Gertrude and Willow priced donated clothing and took it out to the racks. Gertrude couldn't believe there were enough people in Mattawooptock to donate this much clothing. Where had it all come from?

Gertrude's feet hurt. She was actually considering abandoning the investigation, and her new job, when Willow declared a smoke break.

"I don't smoke," Gertrude said, confused.

"But I do," Willow said, and left the room.

Thank God, Gertrude thought, and scurried over to the final bin.

But there was nothing in it. Nothing but clothing and one clown puppet with half of its glass face shattered. Gertrude shuddered and buried the clown in clothes. *Where on earth could that damnable lamp be?* Gertrude wondered, looking around. Then, with a sinking feeling, she realized it could be in one of the recycling boxes. These were huge. And tall. She looked around for something to stand on and was relieved to see that someone had donated a small, wooden bookcase. She dragged it over to the glass recycling box and leaned on it, putting all her weight on it to make sure it was sturdy. It appeared to be. Then, very carefully, she climbed the bookshelf like a stepladder, and, clinging to the edge of the box, peered into the glass recycling. There was a lot of it, but as she scanned each inch of the pile, she became confident she could see nary a shade of green.

"What are you doing?" Willow barked from behind her, startling her. She wheeled around, trying to look innocent, but as her left foot came off the bookshelf, it began to wobble under the weight of her right foot. Just then a loud bell sounded, further startling Gertrude.

"Ahhh!" she cried, afraid of plummeting to her death in front of the minivan that had just pulled up to donate more puzzles.

Willow ran to her and steadied the bookcase so that Gertrude could climb down, which she did, gingerly placing one hand on Willow's shoulder for support. Willow's grimace made it clear that she was barely tolerating that hand.

"Thank you," Gertrude said, when she had returned to the safe cement and leaned on her walker with both hands. "Much obliged."

"I repeat, what were you doing?"

"I, um, I … accidentally dropped my ring in there." Willow didn't look convinced. "I think," Gertrude added.

"You dropped your ring in a box that is taller than you are?"

"It is not," Gertrude snapped, and then realized that was beside the point. "Well, I was throwing something in there and my ring flew off. I thought it went in there."

Willow looked skeptically at Gertrude's hands.

"What?" Gertrude asked, afraid to look down.

"You're wearing rubber gloves."

Gertrude looked down at her hands. "Oh. Yeah. I guess I am."

Willow rolled her eyes again. "You know what? I don't care what you were doing. Let's get back to work."

Gertrude and Willow finished the clothes and then moved on to book pricing, which bored Gertrude to death. "I didn't know this many people read books," she said at one point.

"Again," Willow responded, "I'm not surprised."

The book pricing and stocking took them right to five o'clock.

"Time to go," Willow said, sounding relieved.

"I'm going to stay just a bit longer," Gertrude said.

"Absolutely not," Willow said. "If anyone is going to get extra hours, it's not going to be you."

Gertrude furrowed her brow, confused for a second. Then, "Oh. Right. Extra hours. Yeah. That's what I wanted."

Willow looked puzzled, but she turned to go. "Come on, let's go clock out."

There was no actual process for clocking out. They just told Sherri they were leaving.

"How did it go?" Sherri asked.

Willow and Gertrude answered at the same time: "Oh, about what you'd expect" and "Great!" respectively.

Sherri smiled. "Good to hear. See you both tomorrow."

When Gertrude saw that Willow was really leaving, she turned around. Sherri glanced at her. "Just forgot something in the back. I'm going to go fetch it," Gertrude offered. Sherri nodded and turned to help a customer.

Gertrude returned to the back room and was relieved to find it empty. She dragged the bookcase back into position and climbed up to peer into the electronics box, which was nearly empty. She didn't need the bookshelf for the computers box. That one was much smaller. Nothing. Then she climbed back up to look into the paper and cardboard box. Again, mostly empty. She was starting to get cocky when she climbed up to look into the clothing box. Then she groaned. It was chock-full. Just then, Matt entered the back room through the swinging doors. Without thinking much about what she was doing, Gertrude hoisted one leg onto the box and then rolled into the pile of rejected clothing. Not impressed with the way the pile smelled, she instinctively sat up, but then thought better of it. He might see her head pop up out of the box. So she started to dig. Very carefully. And dig. She had almost dug clear to the bottom when she heard Matt say, "Hey, Roderick. Looks like Willow got everything done for us today. If you want to man the door, I'll go neaten up the floor."

"Sure, Matt," Roderick said.

Gertrude was relieved. She thought it might be easier to sneak past Roderick than Matt. Matt seemed pretty sharp, though probably not as sharp as he seemed to think he was.

As she dug, she found a few things that were probably too good to throw away, and wondered if stealing them from the recycling box was actually stealing. She shook her head to refocus herself. She heard the loud bell again, and seconds later the donation door opened. She felt the blast of cold air from inside the box, and welcomed the fresh smell of it. There was some rustling, more footsteps, and then she heard Roderick say, "Sorry, sir. We can't take that kind of television."

Then she heard a stranger cuss out Roderick. She was thinking about climbing out to jump to his defense, but before she could make up her mind, the man stomped off. He must have dropped something else off though, because within a few minutes, a large pair of dingy women's underwear landed on her left hand. She stifled a scream. Then she dodged a pair of one legged jeans that soared into the box.

She felt through every inch of that box, but there was no lamp. Disappointed, she began to think about climbing out of the box. She could still hear Roderick moving around, but she was willing to bet he wasn't very observant.

She was wrong.

When she poked her head out of the box to have a look, Roderick screamed like a Stephen King prom queen. This frightened Gertrude so, she screamed right back.

Roderick stopped screaming. "How long have you been in there?"

"Oh, just a minute," Gertrude said. "Accidentally dropped my ring in here." She was no longer wearing rubber gloves, so now this lie was far more plausible.

Gertrude looked down and noticed that Roderick had moved the bookcase. "Where's the bookcase?" she asked. Then she noticed her walker was missing too. "Where's my walker?"

"Oh, sorry," Roderick said. "I thought it was donated—"

"Where is it?" she demanded, her panic escalating.

"Out on the floor," he said, looking terrified.

"Go get it!" she screeched.

A woman she didn't recognize came flying through the swinging doors. "What's going on?" she asked and then noticed Gertrude sitting in the box of recycled clothing. "Who are you?" she asked.

"Who are you?" Gertrude countered.

"I'm Rose, the night manager."

"Oh. I'm Gertrude."

No one else said anything. Roderick was staring at the floor as if he'd been caught in something shameful.

"What was all the screaming about?" Rose asked. "And why are you in a recycling box?"

"I'm looking for my missing ring, and this birdbrain is trying to sell my walker!"

Rose looked dumbfounded. "Do you work here?" she asked Gertrude.

"No. I mean, yes. Started today. Can you please tell him to go get my walker, before someone buys it? Everything I own is in that walker pouch!" This was a small exaggeration.

Rose looked at Roderick. "Did you put her walker out on the floor?"

Roderick nodded. "I didn't know it was hers."

"Can you please go get it?"

Roderick nodded again and then left.

"So," Rose said, looking at Gertrude, "can you climb out of there?"

"Sure," Gertrude said, as if that was obvious, "if you can get me a bookcase or something to stand on."

"How about a stepladder?"

"Oh? We have one of those? Why, sure, that would work just fine."

By the time Roderick returned with her walker, Gertrude had climbed out of the box. She leaned on the walker gratefully, and as she tried to catch her breath, she noticed the price tag. "Ten dollars?" she cried, looking up at Roderick accusingly. "Are you bonkers? Do you know how much I paid for this?"

Roderick didn't answer her. He just looked scared.

"Oh never mind. I have to go home." She was exhausted. And she missed her cats.

As she headed toward the door, she heard Rose ask, "Are you sure she works here?"

8

It was dark when Gertrude arrived home. Grateful for her porch light, she stuck her key into the keyhole, but quickly noticed the door wasn't even locked. She was positive she'd left it locked. She gingerly opened the door and flipped on the lights and was greeted by several glaring felines. She couldn't remember the last time she'd left them alone for so long.

"Sorry, kiddos. Momma's got a job."

Lightning, who was sleeping on a pile of assorted hymnals, licked his paw snobbishly in response.

Gertrude looked around. At first, nothing seemed to be amiss, but then she noticed that a new path had been carved toward the corner of her living room where she kept her rock collections. She gasped. She felt angry, scared, and violated all at once. As she entered the new path, she couldn't stand the way things had been thrown about, all willy-nilly, so she began to reorganize as she went. The perpetrator had put records on top of her eight-track bins, and that almost pushed her over the edge. She moved the records back to their proper place and then refolded all the afghans that had been tossed onto her stacks of mason jars. When she had left home, her afghans had been neatly folded and stacked according to color in correspondence to the rainbow, leaning against her favorite hutch, which was full of decorative plates and butter dishes. She was so grieved by the mess of afghans, it took her several minutes to notice that the hutch stood open. A few butter dishes appeared to have been moved—she could tell by smudges in the dust, but nothing appeared to be missing. *This is the weirdest break-in ever.*

She finished refolding and reorganizing, fed her cats, and then put her coat back on and headed out into the cold.

She pounded on Calvin's door.

"What?" he hollered over the noise of his television. She heard a burst of gunfire and figured he must be watching another western. She didn't really enjoy westerns unless they featured Wild Bill Hickok. Something about that man just got her motor running.

She tried the doorknob. It was locked this time. *That sneaky scoundrel!*

"Calvin, open up! Someone broke into my trailer again," she hollered through the door.

The gunfire stopped and she heard footsteps. Calvin opened the door. "I thought you were locking your door these days?" he asked.

She pushed by him. "I did, obviously. I didn't just fall off the turnip truck, you know. Of course I lock my door. But someone must have picked the lock. Or used a key. I don't know how they did it. I just know that when I got home, my door was unlocked and someone had messed up my afghan pile."

Calvin closed his door. "A key? Where would someone get a key? And why would someone steal an afghan, Gert?"

"Don't call me Gert, and I don't know where they got a key. And I didn't say someone stole an afghan. I just said they messed with my pile. As far as I can tell, they didn't take anything. They just rifled through it. So did you see anything? Anyone suspicious in the neighborhood?"

"No, Gertrude. I've been watching television with the curtains drawn. I work pretty hard at *not* seeing anything that goes on in this neighborhood."

"Oh, Calvin. Stop acting like you're too good to live in a trailer park. You *do* live in a trailer park, you know. Anyway, you haven't been watching TV *all* day. I don't know when this thug broke in. Could have been this morning for all I know."

"You've been gone all day?" Calvin exclaimed, incredulous. "Why? Where were you?"

"I got a job."

Calvin laughed. "No. Really."

"It's not funny. I got a job."

"As in someone actually *hired* you to investigate something?"

"No, as in I got a real job. At Goodwill."

"Oh!" Calvin exclaimed as if suddenly everything made sense. "So you're hiring yourself to figure out who killed that young woman?"

"I didn't *hire myself*," Gertrude said. "But yes, I'm going to solve Tislene Breen's murder. I already know more than the cops do."

"Of course you do," Calvin said, and walked back to his recliner. He sat down. "So maybe the break-in is connected to your current investigation?"

"Oh!" she said thoughtfully. "I hadn't thought of that."

"You hadn't thought of that? Why else would someone break into your trailer? Do you have anything worth stealing?"

"I have lots of stuff worth stealing. You should see my jewelry collection!"

"Gertrude, if you buy jewelry at a lawn sale, it's probably not worth stealing."

"Look, did you see anything or not?"

"Not."

"Fine," she said, turning toward the door. "Well, would you keep the curtains open tomorrow? I've got to go to work again."

Calvin reclined. "Yeah, that's usually how jobs work. You have to go to them more than once."

9

Willow met Gertrude at the door. "You're late."

"No, I'm not," Gertrude said, taking off her coat.

Willow pointed at the clock. "It's past nine."

Gertrude looked at the clock. "Oh bosh. It's two minutes past nine. Anyway, I have a good reason for being a few seconds late." Gertrude waited for Willow to ask, but she didn't. So Gertrude told her anyway. "I had to booby-trap my trailer before I left this morning. Then my cats sprung half the traps, and I had to start all over."

Willow wisely avoided this topic of conversation. "Whatever. Come on, someone practically destroyed the plus-sized section. We've got to go organize."

Willow wasn't kidding. Someone had definitely made a mess of the full-figured items. "What in tarnation?" Gertrude asked.

"I know. I wonder the same thing. I guess people think that because the stuff is used, they can treat it like it has no value?" She bent over to pick up a zebra-striped cami and put it back on a hanger.

Gertrude followed her lead and began to pick up the many items that had fallen off or been knocked off the rack. She tired of this after the third time she bent over, so she let Willow do the heavy lifting and she began to simply neaten up the hanging blouses. As she did this, she noticed a flurry of activity in the row of large blouses. "What's she up to?"

Willow rolled her eyes. "Oh, we kind of just let Azalea do what she wants to do. She is currently organizing blouses by color. It's annoying, but it makes her happy. I'll have to go through later and make sure she didn't screw up the sizing while she was making her rainbow."

Gertrude scowled. "What do you have against rainbows? I happen to like rainbows."

"I'm sure you do."

Gertrude was wondering what she'd meant by that when she noticed two uniforms enter the store. She groaned.

"What?" Willow asked, looking up.

"The cops are here."

"So?"

"So, I really don't like Hale."

"Who's Hale?"

"The handsome one."

Willow giggled, and Gertrude looked at her, shocked.

"What?" Willow asked.

"I didn't know you knew how to laugh. Or smile, come to think of it."

"Oh, shut up," Willow snapped, her giggle long gone.

Gertrude watched the two deputies speak to Sherri up front by the registers. Then Sherri led them toward the back. Gertrude's eyes followed them all the way through the swinging doors. When she could no longer see them, her feet decided to give chase. Slowly.

"Where do you think you're going?" Willow asked.

"I'm going to go see what they're up to. They're probably finally looking for the murder weapon. I've got to tell them where I've already searched. Don't want them to waste their time."

"Get back here!" Willow commanded, but Gertrude was already gone.

She pushed through the swinging doors just in time to see the police escorting Roderick out through the back. In handcuffs. Sherri watched him go, and then turned around and saw Gertrude gawking. "Back to work," she said, firmly, but not unkindly.

"Why'd they arrest Roderick?" Gertrude asked.

"It's not our business, Gertrude. Now get back to work, please."

"But was it for the murder? Or something else?"

"The murder," Sherri answered reluctantly. "Now, please?"

Gertrude finally left the back room to rejoin Willow in the now-much-neater plus-sized section. "They just arrested Roderick for the murder," Gertrude exclaimed.

"Humph. Not surprised. That guy's a weirdo."

"Yeah, but, do you really think he would kill someone? I mean, he's certainly shifty, but he's no murderer," Gertrude said.

"How do you know? I think we're done here. At least I'm done. You haven't really done much of anything. Go dust off the glassware."

"Why? Where are you going?" Gertrude asked, excited about the idea of being left alone.

"I'm going to go ask Sherri if she wants me to cover the back. I guess Roderick won't be accepting donations today."

As Gertrude headed toward the glassware aisle, she heard whimpering in the Christmas section. She headed that way, and found Azalea standing in front of a plastic Christmas tree, crying. Wondering how she could have already learned of Roderick's arrest, Gertrude said, "There, there, Azalea. It doesn't mean he did it. The police are still investigating. They'll figure out that he's innocent. They're just slow is all."

Azalea looked up, confused. "What? Who is innocent?"

Gertrude was baffled. "Why are you crying?"

Azalea sniffed and then wiped her nose on her sleeve. Gertrude reached into her walker pouch and pulled out a Burger King napkin. She stepped forward to hand it to Azalea, and then stepped back to remain a safe distance from Azalea's emotions. Azalea took the napkin and made an obvious effort to catch her breath. "This Christmas tree has a thirty-dollar price tag on it."

Gertrude looked at the plastic tree and then back at Azalea. "So?"

"So!" Azalea cried. "This tree doesn't cost thirty dollars! It only cost two dollars! Yesterday, it only cost two dollars!"

Gertrude scowled at her. "Why are you crying?" she repeated.

Azalea looked at her, wide-eyed. "Someone switched the tags!" she cried. "Someone bought something that was supposed to cost thirty dollars! And they only paid two dollars!"

"Oh," Gertrude said. She looked at the tree. Then she looked at Azalea again. "So?"

Azalea was overcome with a whole new round of hysterics. "Oh, never mind! You don't understand! Nobody ever understands!" she cried, and ran for the bathroom.

Gertrude didn't exactly care about Azalea's weird emotional breakdown, but she also didn't want to dust wine goblets, so she headed toward the front to look for Sherri. She soon found her.

"Sherri, something is wrong with Azalea," Gertrude said, trying to display a concerned expression.

"What happened?" Sherri asked, her eyes scanning the store.

"She was crying in the Christmas aisle," Gertrude said. "Something about switched price tags."

"Oh," Sherri said, as if that explained everything. "Where did she go?"

"Bathroom," Gertrude said, and Sherri headed that way. "What, does Christmas make everyone bonkers around here?" she asked the back of Sherri's head.

"This is nothing. You should see Halloween," Sherri said without turning around.

Gertrude still didn't want to dust the glass aisle, so she headed to the back. Willow was standing with her head out the donation door, smoking. When she saw Gertrude, she hurriedly stomped out her cigarette and tried to look casual.

"I just found Azalea sobbing over a switched price tag. Is that normal?" Gertrude asked.

Willow smirked. "Yeah. Normal for her. I'm telling you, she lives and breathes this place. She takes it personally if someone shoplifts. Once, someone wrote a naughty word on the bathroom door, and she was inconsolable for a week."

Gertrude stared at her, thinking about Azalea.

"What?" Willow asked self-consciously.

"Nothing," Gertrude said. "So, any new donations of interest?"

"Nope. Most stuff comes in on the weekends."

"So you just stand here all day doing nothing?"

Willow gave her a dirty look. "No, I sort and price while I'm back here. We don't really need to stand by the door. When someone drives up, an alarm sounds back here."

"Oh yeah, I've heard that bell. I wondered what that was."

"Yeah, well now you know. Did you dust the glassware?"

"Of course! Who was back here during the murder?"

"What?"

"Who was back here," Gertrude repeated slowly, "when Tislene Breen was killed?"

"I was," Willow snapped. "Why? What does that have to do with anything?"

"And there was no one else? Nobody dropping things off? I mean, you would've heard them when they pulled up, right?"

Willow looked suspicious. "Yes. I suppose. But there wasn't anyone. I was all alone. I didn't even know something had happened until the cops came to talk to me."

10

Gertrude didn't have to work on the weekend, but still she called the CAP bus first thing Saturday morning.

When the large van pulled up in front of her trailer, she was disheartened to see that Andrea was driving. Andrea took her job a little too seriously, in Gertrude's opinion.

"Destination?" Andrea said as Gertrude slid into the van.

"County jail," Gertrude answered.

Andrea turned toward her and looked at her suspiciously. "I can only take you to necessary stops. Why do you need to go to the jail?"

"I need to pay a fine," Gertrude lied.

"Fines are paid at the courthouse," Andrea said, unblinkingly.

"You know what?! You need to get a life!" Gertrude cried.

"And you need to get a driver's license!" Andrea gave it right back.

"I can't. I'm disabled."

Andrea turned around in her seat and stared out the windshield. "You can get out now. I'm not taking you to the jail. Why on earth would you want to go to the jail anyway?"

Gertrude gritted her teeth. Then she said, slowly, emphatically, and not a little menacingly, "I need to go to the jail because I'm having a steamy affair with a hardened criminal who happens to be staying there right now. If you don't take me to him, right now, I will tell him that you are the reason I missed our date. I will tell him where you live and I will make sure he pays you a visit when he gets out."

Andrea looked at her in the rearview mirror. She didn't look convinced. She also looked a little scared. Wordlessly, she put the van in drive and headed toward the jail. The two women stayed silent for the ride, and for disembarkation. Gertrude noted, with some satisfaction, that Andrea did not log this particular ride on her infuriatingly neat clipboard.

Gertrude entered the clean lobby of the Somerset County Jail and wondered at what a nice place it was. It looked more like an office building than a jail, and the large welcome desk sat empty before her. She rang the call bell. No one materialized. She rang it again. And again. Soon, an annoyed-looking young man in uniform appeared. "Can I help you?" he asked tersely.

"I'm here to visit one of your prisoners."

The man sat down. "No visitations on weekends." He pointed to a sign on the counter that read just that.

"Oh doodlebug!" Gertrude exclaimed.

The man frowned.

"So I have to wait till Monday?"

The man nodded, still frowning. "And you'll need to have an appointment," he said, pointing at the sign again, which also included this information.

"Fine. Then I need to make an appointment please," Gertrude said.

"All right," the man said, and tapped a few keys on the computer in front of him. "And who would you like to visit?"

"Roderick."

The man looked up. "Roderick who?"

"I don't know," Gertrude admitted.

"Well, we need a last name in order to schedule an appointment."

"Oh piffle! How many Rodericks were arrested for murder yesterday?"

A look of recognition flashed across the guard's face. "I'm sorry, I'll need a last name. Then I'd be happy to schedule an appointment."

Gertrude stood up straight. "You know who I'm talking about!"

Without looking at her, he said, "I don't know anything."

Gertrude walked to the door and called the CAP bus again.

"That was a quick visit," Andrea muttered as Gertrude slid into the van.

"He's a man of few words," Gertrude said.

"Where to now? The casino?"

"There's a casino in Mattawooptock?" Gertrude asked, appalled.

"That was a joke. Where do you want to go, your highness?"

Having absolutely no idea why Andrea had just called her "your highness," she said, "Church please. Open Door."

Andrea did as she was asked and looked quite relieved when Gertrude climbed out of the van in the church parking lot.

Gertrude hurried inside and out of the cold. She hung her coat in the lobby and then headed into the office. "Hi, Maggie. Hi, Tiny," she greeted her friends.

"Hey, Gert. What brings you here?" Maggie asked brightly.

"Need to talk to Pastor Dan," Gertrude said.

"He's in his office," Maggie said, nodding at his office door.

Gertrude went in without knocking and plopped down in a chair without being invited.

"Hey, Gert. Haven't seen you in a few Sundays. Everything OK?" Pastor Dan asked.

"Yes. Sorry. Been busy as a bee in springtime. Anyway, I need you to go see a friend of mine."

"OK," Pastor Dan said. Then he waited. Gertrude didn't say anything else. "Who is this friend?"

"His name is Roderick. He was arrested yesterday for murdering Tislene Breen, that woman they found in Goodwill? But he didn't do it. So, he's in jail, and they won't let me in to see him. So I was hoping I could go with you. You know, sort of like a pastor's assistant. I think they'd let you in. Must be a human right or something, right? They can't deny him spiritual counsel?"

Pastor Dan laughed. "First of all, yes they can. Second, they won't let me in on weekends. Third, I'm not taking an assistant in. Why are you so motivated to see him? Is this a good friend?"

"Not really. I hardly know him. But I need to know why they arrested him. I need to know what sort of evidence they have against him."

"Ah!" Pastor said, as if he suddenly understood the whole conversation. "And why do you need to know this?"

"So that I can figure out who really did it."

"Why don't you just let the police handle this, Gertrude? I say this as your pastor and as your friend. I don't want you to get hurt."

"Look, will you go visit him or not?"

"Of course. But if he tells me something about his situation, I'm not going to share that with you."

Gertrude stood up quickly and glared at the pastor she loved. "Fine then." She turned and stomped toward the door.

Pastor Dan called after her. "I'll still plan to visit him on Monday. What'd you say his last name was?"

11

Gertrude was feeling discouraged when she walked into Goodwill on Monday morning. She wasn't making much progress on this case, and had accomplished essentially nothing over the weekend except a steady stream of circular thought. But what bothered her most was her certainty of Roderick's innocence, and she couldn't stand not knowing why the cops thought he was guilty.

Sherri greeted her when she walked into the store. "Willow's in the back. Go find her, and she'll put you to work."

Gertrude nodded somberly. On her way to the swinging doors, she passed Azalea, who was rearranging DVDs.

"What are you doing?" Gertrude asked, a little more crankily than she'd meant to.

"I'm putting the movies in alphabetical order."

"Why?"

"Because it looks nice," Azalea explained.

Gertrude continued toward the back and was met at the swinging doors by Willow.

"You're late again," she scolded.

"Booby-traps," Gertrude explained.

"I think that term is offensive to women," Matt declared from a bin to their right.

Willow glared at him. "Eavesdropping is also offensive to women. And booby-traps have nothing to do with breasts. Good grief, Matt. Get a life!"

Matt swore at her, but Willow ignored him.

"Come on, Gertrude. We don't have time for him. Today is pull day. We've got lots of work to do."

"What in tarnation is a pull day?" Gertrude asked.

"Every Monday is pull day. We switch the tag color today."

Gertrude stared at her blankly.

"So, you might not have noticed," Willow began, speaking patronizingly slowly, "that all week yellow-barbed items have been half-off. On Mondays, that changes. Today, red stuff went half-price. So we have to go through and pull all the yellow-tagged stuff off the shelves."

"Oh!" Gertrude exclaimed, actually excited. "And what do we do with the yellow stuff?"

"It goes to Gorham," Willow said. "Come on, we'll start in toys. There's usually not much stuff left there." Willow began to push an empty blue bin toward the toys.

"What's Gorham?" Gertrude asked, following her.

"Gorham, Maine," Willow said, reverting to her condescending tone.

"I know that," Gertrude snapped. "But why do we send stuff to Gorham? What's there? A Goodwill bargain barn?"

"No. The pound store."

"The *pound store*?" Gertrude repeated. She felt her heart rate increase at the very words. "What exactly is a pound store?"

Willow parked the bin and began picking through the toys. "It's exactly what it sounds like. You can buy this stuff and pay for it by the pound."

"You're kidding!" Gertrude could suddenly think of nothing else but getting herself to this pound store.

Willow stared at her. "Are you going to help or not?"

Gertrude began to push the puzzles around, but she wasn't really looking at the tags. "So what happens? They have scales at the checkout?"

"Yep."

"Wowsa," Gertrude said. Despite her lack of attention, a yellow price tag jumped out at her. She pulled the Scrabble game from its shelf. "This has a yellow sticker. So it goes to Gorham now?"

"Yes," Willow said, as if she were talking to someone incredibly stupid. "Now you put it in this here bin," she said.

Gertrude dropped it in. Then suddenly she exclaimed, "Oh Mylanta!" so loudly that Willow actually jumped.

"What?" she cried. "Did you see a spider?"

"That's it!" Gertrude cried, and then looked around for a spider.

"What's it?"

"How does the stuff get to Gorham?"

"A truck."

"When does the truck come?" she asked breathlessly.

"I don't know. Sometime Monday night. Why does it matter?"

"Because that's where the lamp must have gone."

"What lamp?" Willow asked, reasonably enough.

"The ugly green dead-bird-lamp! It wasn't in any of the bins, or any of the recycling boxes, or any of the trash cans, or the dumpster, and it was so big, someone would have noticed if someone tried to walk out of the store with it—"

"What lamp?" Willow barked.

Gertrude looked at her. "Will you drive me to the pound store?"

Willow laughed. "What? Like right now?"

"Yes! It's a matter of life and death!"

"The life and death of a lamp?" Willow asked.

"Of course not!" Gertrude snapped. "Will you take me or not?"

Willow laughed again. "You're nuts. I'm at work. *You're* at work, for that matter. We can't just take off. And even if we could, I wouldn't take you. Do you know how far Gorham is?"

"I need a smoke break," Gertrude said, and turned and headed toward the bathroom. She had no intention of smoking, obviously, but that excuse seemed to work for others, and she needed some alone time to think. How was she going to get to Gorham? It had to be a hundred miles away. She didn't even want to think about how much that would cost in a taxi.

Calvin. It had to be him. He was the only option. Her only chance. But how was she going to convince him to drive her to Gorham?

She left the bathroom and headed toward the back to grab her coat. Then she called the CAP bus. She thought about leaving through the donation door, but didn't want Sherri to worry that the murderer had struck again, so she headed up front.

Sherri was checking out a customer. "I have to go," Gertrude said.

"Why?" Sherri called out as Gertrude headed for the door.

"Sorry, can't explain. It's an emergency."

She hurried out into the cold and then stopped three feet from the door to wait. She breathed a visible sigh of relief when she saw Norman behind the wheel. She threw herself into the van.

"You OK, Gertrude? You seem a little, well, flushed."

"I'm fine, Norm," she said and slammed the door behind her. "Don't suppose you can drive me to Gorham?"

"Gorham? Why?"

"Can you or can't you?"

"Well, no, I don't think so. I mean, if you had some sort of medical appointment, we could probably get you a ride, but I'd have to talk to my supervisor."

"No, never mind. There's no time. Just take me home."

When they stopped in front of her trailer, she was alarmed to see her front door ajar. She leapt out of the van and made a beeline for her steps, but as she ascended them, she met Calvin coming out of her trailer.

"Calvin!" she exclaimed. "What in tarnation are you doing?"

"I saw her!" he exclaimed right back.

"Saw who?"

"The burglar! I called the cops. They should be here any second, but I didn't want to wait. I wanted to catch her in the act, but she went out a window."

Gertrude pushed past him into her trailer. She looked down at the mess on her floor. "What happened here?"

"What happened is, you didn't tell me you had the place rigged, and I came running in here and fell flat on my fanny! That's what happened!" He turned around to show her that his entire backside was covered in baby powder.

"Aw shucks, Calvin! I was trying to capture the culprit's footprint!"

"Well, you may have, but then I wiped it out. You could have picked something less slippery! I'm only wearing my moccasins. Not exactly hiking treads."

"OK, but you saw her?"

"Indeed, I did. As I was flopping around in your Blue Rose Talcum powder, I saw her go out through that window," he said, pointing.

Gertrude walked over to the window, which was still open. The perpetrator had apparently climbed over her recliner to get out the window. She gasped. "Calvin, look!"

Calvin started across the room to her and then stopped. "Are there any other traps I should be aware of? Maybe a landmine or deadfall?"

"Don't be ridiculous. Just watch out for that tripwire, right there," she said, pointing.

"What's that do?"

"Sets off an air horn," Gertrude explained.

"What's an air horn going to do?"

"Hopefully scare the snot right out of the bad guy! Now, get over here and look at this."

He crossed the room and looked at her find: a perfect imprint of the front half of a shoe, as if the intruder had pushed off the recliner to get out through the window. "Well, I'll be darned. It worked, sort of."

"Yep! I'll say!" Gertrude took her phone out and snapped several pictures of the footprint, as they both heard approaching sirens.

Calvin met the deputies at the door. "Watch your step," he said. "It's a mite slick right here."

Hale entered and looked down at the white powder all over the floor. "Uh …" he started, but then he looked up and saw Gertrude. "Oh great."

"Don't oh great me, you meanieface! Someone has broken into my house *multiple* times, and I guarantee you it is the same person who killed Tislene Breen. They're after me now because I'm hot on their tail."

"Don't you mean trail?" Hale said.

Gertrude ignored him.

"Are you sure it's the same culprit?" Calvin asked. "A few months ago, you were sure your prowler was the stripper from your last case."

Gertrude smiled at his use of the word "case."

"If it's happened multiple times, why haven't you called us?" Hale asked. "Why haven't you filed a report? And why are you smiling?"

"Because I have done your job, again!" Gertrude declared. She dragged a tote into place and climbed atop it so she could reach for something on her piano.

"Careful!" Calvin said. "Do you need me to get something? Maybe a safety harness?"

"Got it!" Gertrude cried triumphantly, as she dropped back to the floor with a crash. She handed a small camera to Hale. "This is motion-activated. You might have to watch some cats moving about, but it should also tell you exactly who broke in. Now, if you'll dust the place for prints"—Hale looked around wonderingly—"I'll leave you to it. Calvin and I have to get to Gorham, STAT!"

"Where did you get such a thing?" Hale asked, looking over the camera. He looked impressed.

"Cabela's Bargain Cave," Gertrude said. "It's for wildlife. But I don't really care much for wildlife." And with that, Gertrude headed out of the trailer, expecting Calvin to follow, which he did.

"Do you know if anything is missing?" Hale called after her.

"Watch the tape! See if she took anything!" Gertrude called back. "We've got to go!"

A few seconds later, Gertrude and Calvin heard the air horn go off.

12

"You wanna tell me why we're going to Gorham?" Calvin asked.

"I can't."

"Why not?"

"Because then you might not go."

"Well how about this. If you *don't* tell me, I won't go."

Gertrude looked at him. "You're already going."

Calvin looked exasperated. "I can turn this car around, Gertrude. Just tell me where we're going."

Gertrude thought about it. *He's a snob. He's going to think a pound store is beneath him. But if I don't tell him, he might not help me.* "I know what the murder weapon was," she announced. "And I think I know where to find it."

He looked interested. "Where?"

"In Gorham."

"Gertrude!" he hollered.

"You don't have to holler. We're in a small space here."

"Where in Gorham?!" he hollered.

She sighed and then mumbled, "The pound store."

"The what?"

"It's where Goodwill treasures go to die. They call it the pound store because people pay by the pound. I think the murderer put it in the bin that was bound for the pound store. Hey, that rhymed!"

Calvin thought for a minute, but he didn't slow down or touch his turn signal, for which Gertrude was grateful. "So then, the murderer must work at Goodwill."

"Right. Probably. They already arrested Roderick, but I don't think he did it."

"Why not?" Calvin asked.

"Because I asked him if he did, and he said he didn't."

"You know, Gertrude. Sometimes people do this thing called lying. I know you are entirely unfamiliar with such a practice," he said sarcastically.

"Nah," she answered. "I lie quite a bit. So I can usually tell when someone else is lying. Unless they're really good at it. And I don't think Roderick is good at much of anything."

"And I'm assuming that you told the police about your Gorham theory?" Calvin asked.

"I tried."

"All right then. Let's go to the pound store. What's the murder weapon?"

"It is the ugliest green lamp you've ever seen. And it had dead birds hanging off it. Well, they weren't really dead. They just looked it. Hang on," she said and flipped over to reach into the back.

"I hate it when you do this," Calvin said, leaning toward the door. "I don't like being this close to your bottom."

She flopped back into her seat. "Here," she said, showing him the bird. "I found this. It fell off the lamp. But there were a whole bunch of other birds hanging off it too. I'm telling you, we find this lamp, there will be no mistaking it."

"OK and then what?"

"What do you mean, and then what? Then we have the murder weapon!" Gertrude said.

"Yeah, but Gertrude, it's going to have a million fingerprints on it by now."

"Oh yeah, well, I guess I hadn't thought of it. Let's just hope it *doesn't* have Roderick's prints on it. That will help him. And even if it's got a million prints on it, at least it will narrow down the suspect pool to a million."

Calvin laughed. "Great. Hale will be thrilled."

Gertrude slept most of the way to Gorham, and awoke disoriented when Calvin poked her.

"What?" she said, and then wiped a bit of drool from her lip.

"Get out your phone. We need the GPS."

"Oh. All right. Why didn't you just say so?"

"I just did."

Gertrude opened her map app and then began to slowly type.

"What are you giving it for a destination?" Calvin asked.

"Pound store."

"That's not going to work. You need an add—"

"It just did work," Gertrude interrupted as the map appeared.

"You are on the fastest route," Gertrude's phone declared.

Calvin grunted.

"Holy smokes," he said when they pulled into the large parking lot. "Why are there so many people here?"

"I don't know," Gertrude said, looking around in wonder. "We'd better get in there. It never occurred to me that someone might actually buy the stupid thing, but who knows with this many people here."

"All right. Let's go, before I change my mind," Calvin said and climbed out of the car.

Gertrude's legs had stiffened up during the long ride, but Calvin walked slowly alongside her as they made their way to the front door. This made her feel warm and fuzzy inside.

When they entered the dimly lit room, Calvin let out a low whistle. "This is so disturbing."

Gertrude couldn't believe her eyes. The pound store was a warehouse. A warehouse full of blue bins. And there were so many people. Scores of them surrounding each blue bin, digging with diligence.

"How are we ever going to find anything in here?" Gertrude asked, a little worried.

"We should split up," Calvin suggested. Gertrude didn't like the idea, but she knew he was right. "I'll go left. You go right. Good luck," and he was off.

Gertrude made her way to the right. And she began to dig along with the rest of them. She noticed most of the diggers were wearing rubber gloves and she sincerely regretted not bringing some. As she contemplated this, a man elbowed her hard in the ribs. "Oh!" she cried accusingly. She gave him a glare, but then saw he was holding a hammer and got scared. She moved to the other side of the bin, but no matter how she went at it, someone was always pushing her out of the way.

She noticed a long line of shopping carts along the wall and she headed toward these. Most of them were overflowing with goodies. She began to paw through one of them but a woman began screaming at her in a language other than her own. She backed away from the cart and realized many people were staring at her. *Oh no.* She realized then that these carts belonged to shoppers. They were filled with treasures that had already been claimed. She walked back to the bins, but when people stopped staring at her, she meandered toward the carts again. She resolved not to paw through them, but it couldn't hurt to look, right? In the last cart, she saw something that made her heart leap. Keeping one eye on the crowd, she sneakily rearranged the cart until she could get a good look at the lamp inside it. But alas, it was the wrong lamp. No dead birds.

Just then, a tired-looking employee pushed a new, full bin toward her. She happily scurried toward it.

"Back!" someone barked. She looked around for the source of the command. Then she found her. Another angry woman was glaring at her. "Back! Stay behind the line!" she ordered. Gertrude looked down at her feet and sure enough, there was an actual red line on the floor. She stepped back behind it and waited, along with a growing crowd. Then the drill sergeant yelled, "OK, go!" and the crowd attacked the new bin. If it weren't for her walker, Gertrude certainly would have been trampled. She watched the experts dig in and waited for some of the mania to abate before perusing the bin herself.

Nothing.

The next bin: nothing.

The next bin: a gorgeous sparkly purple housecoat she just had to have.

The next bin: an Elvis pepper shaker. There was no salt, but she figured that was OK. It was the King, after all.

The next bin: nothing.

She stood up and stretched. Her lower back ached like the dickens.

"I don't think it's here, Gertrude," Calvin spoke from behind her.

She turned around. "I know." She felt like crying. "But if it's not here, I don't know where to look next. Someone must have bought it. It could be anywhere in the state by now."

"Or it could be in a landfill. You're right. We've been here for hours. I'm pretty sure I've caught something awful by now. We should go."

"Caught something?" Gertrude asked, sounding hopeful.

"Yeah, as in a communicable disease," Calvin said with a grimace. "Come on, let's go home and take long showers."

"All right," she conceded. "I'm just going to go to the little girls' room first. It's a long ride."

"Fine," he said. "Why not drag this nightmare out some more? I'll go wait by the door."

"Actually," she said, handing him the robe and the Elvis shaker, "can you check out for me? It will save time, and I don't have any money. I'll pay you back later."

"Yeah, when pigs fly," Calvin muttered, but he grudgingly took her finds and headed toward the checkout scales.

She turned and looked around for a restroom sign. She found one that led her down a narrow hallway that spilled out into an even larger warehouse area. Her breath caught as she looked around. This room was triple the size of the one she had just left, and she had thought that one was monstrous. She looked around, her mouth hanging open, and completely forgot about the bathroom. Blue bins were stacked on top of blue bins. In all directions, all she could see was *stuff* stacked up to thirty feet in the air. And then she saw them. Hanging out of a bin. A few dead birds. She made a beeline for that bin and was soon standing under the birds, looking up at them. There was no doubt. They were the same birds. And there was also absolutely no way she could reach them. She looked around for a stepladder or very tall bookcase, but found neither. She did, however, find a forklift.

And the keys were in the ignition.

13

Gertrude climbed up into the machine, her heart thumping madly inside her chest. She turned the key. Then she pressed the gas pedal. Nothing happened. She pressed it harder. Still nothing. She pushed it to the floor and the forklift took off—backward. "Aiiii!" she screeched and slammed on the brakes. Too late, as she slammed into a pile of blue bins behind her. The pile of bins wobbled perilously as she looked up through the overhead guard of the forklift. "Please, Jesus, save me," she whispered as the top few bins teetered off the stack and came careening down on top of her, effectively burying her in last chance Goodwill treasures. She felt something slippery slide by her cheek. She heard glass things smashing on impact. An Elvis salt shaker plopped into her lap.

When everything stopped moving, she checked herself over to make sure she was OK, and found that she was unscathed. Then she heard shouting, but she couldn't see anything except used merchandise. Judging from the sound of footsteps, she figured at least two sets of feet were hurrying toward her.

"I'm all right!" she cried out. "Just had a small accident!"

She heard a flurry of activity, which she assumed was people digging her out, and within minutes, she saw two men, each wearing a blue apron and an incredibly sour expression on his face.

"Who are you?" one of them asked.

"I'm Gertrude."

A woman appeared. "The police are on their way," she said to the men. "They told me not to engage with her."

"The police? Oh, good thinking!" She looked up and was happy to see the dead birds were hanging right where she'd last seen them.

"Can we start picking this up?" one of the men asked.

"Sure," the woman said. "I don't think that would hurt."

Gertrude slyly slid the salt shaker into her pocket, and began to climb out of the forklift.

"You," the woman snapped, looking at her with disdain, "don't move. The police will deal with you."

Gertrude plopped back down in the forklift seat, wishing it had lumbar support.

"I work at Goodwill too," Gertrude said to them. "That means we're practically family."

No one answered her.

The pound store employees had about half of the pile cleared out when two police officers arrived.

"Can you step down out of there, ma'am?" one of them asked.

"Don't call me ma'am. I'm not old," she said. Then she tried to climb down and had some trouble. She looked at the policeman. "Actually, I think I could use a hand."

He politely extended it. Then he said, "I'm Officer Mahoney. This is Officer Fortin."

"I'm Gertrude. Could you retrieve that walker for me?" she asked Officer Fortin. It had been knocked over in the avalanche.

He righted the walker and placed it in front of her. "Thank you. All right. Now, what you're looking for is right up there," she said, pointing to the birds.

Officer Fortin looked. Officer Mahoney did not. He just said, "If you'll follow me, right this way."

"What about the lamp?" Gertrude asked.

"Please don't make this difficult," Mahoney said. "You need to come with us right now."

"Come with you where?" Gertrude asked. She thought it was a reasonable question.

"We're taking you down to the station. These people have to get back to work."

"Oh!" Gertrude said. "Just let me tell Calvin."

"Who's Calvin?" Mahoney asked.

"He's my assistant. And my neighbor. He's out there," she said, pointing to the retail room. "He was checking out for me."

"OK, let's go." Mahoney led the way. Officer Fortin motioned for her to follow Mahoney. They reentered the retail room, and no one paid them any mind, except for Calvin, whose eyes grew wide.

"Can you point him out to us?" Mahoney asked.

She pointed to Calvin and then headed toward him.

"No," Fortin said sternly. "You wait right here. Officer Mahoney will explain the events to him."

Gertrude crossed her arms. "The events? What events? That I crashed a forklift? Look, that was an accident! I was just trying to get the lamp. Look, you just need to call Hale. He's a cop with the Somerset County Sheriff's Department. He'll explain everything to you." She realized Fortin wasn't listening. "Hey!" she cried. She waved a hand in front of his face. "Are you even listening to me?"

Mahoney returned. "OK, I've explained everything to your friend. Now let's go." He grabbed her arm gently but firmly and walked her out to a cruiser that still had its blue lights flashing.

Suddenly, Gertrude felt embarrassed, an emotion she rarely experienced. She wondered for the first time if she was in trouble. Mahoney helped her into the backseat and then collapsed her walker and put it in the trunk. She looked out the window and saw Calvin looking in at her from the doorway. He managed to look both disgusted and concerned.

She tried to roll down the window. Nothing happened. She pounded on it and hollered, "The lamp is back there, Calvin! I saw it! Way up high! You need to go get it! It's back there! In a blue bin! The dead birds are showing!"

"Quiet!" Mahoney ordered as he slid into the driver's seat.

Gertrude remained silent and still, but she was fuming. *This is what I get for trying to catch a murderer! How was I supposed to know the forklift was broken? Why in tarnation did it go backward? And why won't anyone listen to me?*

They pulled into the Gorham Police Department, and Mahoney helped Gertrude out of the car. Then he led her to a small room and offered her a chair. She accepted. She expected him to sit down too, but he left her there, alone. She was exhausted. She was starving. She was frustrated. And she missed her cats so much that she vowed to never leave her house again. Then she thought she probably ought to still go to church. But that was it. House and church. Thinking about church made her think about Pastor Dan. He was always getting people out of trouble.

Officer Fortin entered the small room and sat down.

"Can I have a phone call?"

"Not right now. You're not under arrest."

"I'm not? Then what am I doing here?"

"We just have a few questions."

He asked her for her name and social security number.

She asked him if he had any peanuts.

He did not.

He asked her why she had vandalized the pound store.

"Vandalized? Are you bonkers? I don't vandalize things! I've already tried to tell you. I'm a gumshoe, and I was looking for the murder—"

"A gumshoe?" Fortin interrupted. "Where do you work?"

"Goodwill, but I was at the pound store trying to—"

"Which Goodwill?"

"Mattawooptock."

"OK, and you live in Mattawooptock?"

"Yes. I told you to call Hale—"

"OK, I'll be right back." Officer Fortin disappeared, and Gertrude was alone again. She decided that every interrogation room on earth should have a cat. She vowed that if she ever actually interrogated someone, she would make sure they had a cat to hold.

Officer Fortin reappeared several long minutes later. "You can go, ma'am."

"What?"

"We've talked to your boss, and she explained everything."

"Explained what? She has no idea what I'm—"

"Your friend Calvin is here. He will take you home. But you are not allowed to ever go to the pound store again, OK? Someone could have been seriously hurt. If anyone sees you in the pound store, there will be no more warnings. You'll be in real trouble next time. Do you understand?"

Gertrude nodded.

He stood in the doorway as if waiting for her to get up.

She did. Then she followed Fortin to the lobby and was thrilled to find Calvin waiting there.

"Are you all right?" he asked.

"Just get me out of here, please," Gertrude muttered.

14

In the car, Calvin tried to explain. "Well, the cops think you're a little, well …" he seemed to be searching for the right word.

"A little *what*?" Gertrude snapped.

"Tilted?" he tried.

"Tilted?! Why on earth do they think that?"

"I don't know, but be grateful. They called your boss, and she told them you are disabled, and so they went easy on you. I mean, you're really lucky, Gertrude. You tried to steal a forklift!"

"I didn't steal anything! Well, except the Elvis salt shaker. Did you buy the pepper shaker, by the way?"

"Yes."

"How much was it?"

"Thirteen cents."

"Fabulous," Gertrude said, gleefully. "I'll pay you back."

"Gertrude! Can we talk about what really matters here? Why were you driving a forklift?"

"I found it, Calvin. I tried to tell you through the cop car window. I really found the lamp. It was in the back, but I couldn't reach it. But I found it! It's still there!"

"Are you sure?"

"Dead certain."

Calvin sighed. "Well, I guess you've just got to tell the cops when we get home. I mean, you can't go back in there."

Gertrude was quiet.

"Why are you being quiet? You're making me nervous."

"I'm just tired. And I don't know what to do. I've already tried to tell Hale about the murder weapon, and he ignored me. He made fun of me. I don't want to talk to him again. He's so mean. I really wanted to be the hero, and now I just don't know if that's going to happen."

"Ah," Calvin said, "being the hero is overrated."

"How would you know?"

Calvin chuckled. "I don't. I was just trying to help you feel better."

Gertrude sat alone in her trailer that night. The lights were off, except for the TV, which was on

Antiques Roadshow. Blizzard and Cyclone were curled up on her lap. This was odd, as Cyclone wasn't usually much of a snuggler. She must have sensed that something was amiss.

And something definitely was. Gertrude's determination was flagging. Maybe Calvin was right. Maybe she should just let the cops figure it out. She had tried to help. They had made it clear they didn't want her help. Golly, she disliked Hale. She really wanted to prove him wrong.

A man on the screen was getting an antique headlamp appraised. This gave Gertrude an idea. She stood up abruptly, sending her two feline friends tumbling to the floor. Blizzard landed gracefully and sauntered off. Cyclone gave Gertrude a dirty look and sat down in front of her walker, like a little kitty roadblock.

Gertrude paid her no mind and skirted around her on her way to the kitchen. She flipped on the light over the sink and reached for a box on top of a cupboard. If she remembered correctly, which she always did, the box was full of camping supplies. Gertrude had never been camping in her life, but she was always impressed with those preppers, those folks who were ready for anything. This box was her way of being ready. She pulled out handful after handful of matchbooks, fondly remembering the days when restaurants and stores gave away free matches. They never gave away anything free anymore. She pulled out a water filter, batteries, gauze, latex gloves, antiseptic, fifty feet of rope, a Swiss army knife, a large package of freeze-dried cat food, and then finally, found what she was looking for: an L.L. Bean headlamp. She flipped it on. The batteries still worked. She grabbed a few spare batteries just in case and then slid the big box back into its spot. Then she put the headlamp on her head, put on her coat, and headed out into the cold.

She pounded on Calvin's door.

He didn't answer.

She pounded again. "Calvin!" she hollered as loud as she could.

The door flew open.

"Gertrude! What is wrong with you? It's after midnight!"

"I know! Look!" she said, pointing at her head.

"What?"

"The headlamp!"

"What about it?"

"I was watching *Antiques Roadshow* and I got an idea!"

Calvin stared at her.

"You have to take me back, Calvin. I'll break in. I'll use the headlamp to see. I won't get caught, I promise. I know exactly where the killer lamp is. I'll be in and out, easy-peasy."

"And just how do you plan to break in?" Calvin asked.

"You'll see!" she said, pushing past him into his house. "Come on, put some pants on. We've got to get going so we can be out of there before the sun comes up."

Calvin grudgingly shut the door and followed her into his living room. "Gertrude, I am not, I repeat, I am *not* driving you back to Gorham tonight, or ever for that matter. I don't want you to get into trouble, and even more importantly, *I* don't want to get into trouble. So you go home and go to bed." He turned and headed toward his bedroom. "You can show yourself out. Don't forget to lock the door."

"If you don't take me, I will hitchhike."

Calvin went out of sight, but she heard him grunt. She took a step closer to his dark bedroom. "I swear I will! I will hitchhike!"

"Fine by me. You go have fun," Calvin said. "Try not to get picked up by a serial killer."

It sounded like he had crawled back into bed.

"Fine! Be that way! I'm going! I'm going to hitchhike all the way to Gorham! Maybe I'll live, maybe I won't! Have a nice life, old man!" She turned and stomped down the hall.

She'd gotten all the way to his door when she heard him behind her. "Fine. Just give me a minute to get dressed."

She didn't turn around, so he couldn't see the giant smile spread across her face.

15

Once again, Gertrude slept all the way to Gorham.

Calvin elbowed her in the ribs when he pulled into the now deserted pound store parking lot.

"Ow!" she cried.

"I think I hate you," he said.

"What? Why?"

"Because I'm so tired I think I might die and you just slept for two hours. And this is all your idea."

"Oh yeah. That. Sorry. Tell you what! You can sleep on the way home. I'll drive."

"Fat chance. Are you sure you want to do this?" he asked. "They're going to give you more than a slap on the wrist this time."

"Then let's not get caught," she said.

He parked near the road.

"What are you doing over here? Drive me to the building at least!"

"Gertrude, I don't feel good about this."

"Nothing's going to happen, Calvin. If I get caught, I'll remind them that I am a little *tilted*, remember? Anyway, if they catch me, I'll actually be holding the murder weapon. I'll be a hero."

Calvin didn't look so sure.

"Look if you see blue lights or hear sirens, just drive away. I'll deny you were ever here."

"They're going to know I brought you, Gertrude. How else would you get here? I'm your only friend."

"That's not true! I have lots of friends!" Gertrude cried. *Wait, did he just say we were friends?*

"I think I should go in with you."

Gertrude's eyes grew wide, but it was dark, so he couldn't see that. "All right then. We should get going."

He put the Cadillac in drive and rolled toward the building. "So how were you planning to get into the building?"

"I was going to find a window that wasn't locked."

"That's it? That's your big plan? What if all the windows are locked?"

"Look at this place, Calvin. It's huge. One of the windows will be unlocked, I promise. Sure as mud in mud season."

He pulled up alongside the building and put the car back in park. "I think we have other problems."

"What?" Gertrude asked.

"Well, look. The windows are too high to reach, and they're also ... well, they're fairly *narrow*."

"Well, we can just climb on your car, and what do you mean, narrow?"

"First of all, you're not climbing on my car. Second of all, no offense, but you're not going to fit through that window."

She looked at the window and then she looked down at her own hips. "Maybe you're right. Let's find a bigger window."

"All the windows are the same size, Gertrude."

"Fine. Then what do you suggest? I don't exactly have time to go on a diet."

"I think I should go through the window. Then I'll find my way to the door and let you in."

"Calvin! You're smarter than a whip on Tuesday! You're the best Watson ever."

"Gertrude, if anyone is *Watson*, you are! Now, let's just hope it's unlocked." He held his hand out to her.

She thought about taking it. Then thought better of it. "What?"

"The headlamp."

"Oh," she said and grudgingly handed it over.

He put it on and then got out of the car.

She sat in the car while he climbed onto the roof to check the window. She heard him say a naughty word and within seconds he was back in the driver's seat. "Locked," he said. "Just like I knew it would be."

"Pretty spry for an old guy," she said.

"Shut up." He rubbed his hands together. "Can't believe I'm about to get frostbite for you." He put the car in drive and let it roll to the next window. Then he repeated the process.

After the fifth window, he climbed back into the car out of breath. "I am going to be so lame tomorrow. Probably won't be able to get out of bed."

"You probably won't have to."

The sixth window was the one. "This one's unlocked," he whispered down to her.

"You don't have to whisper," she said. "There's no one here."

"Well excuse me for not knowing how to behave during a robbery."

She heard some grunting and peered up at him as he wrestled with the window. Finally, it slid open. He stuck his head in and peered around.

"What do you see?"

"A bunch of garbage," came the muffled reply. "I'm going in."

Then he bent his knees and jumped toward the window. His feet barely left the roof of the car, but it was enough for him to get his elbows in through the window. Then his legs just sort of dangled there helplessly for several seconds.

"Need a boost?" Gertrude asked.

"You stay off my car!" Calvin snapped, out of breath. He began to rock his body back and forth, and then, inch by inch, he disappeared through the window. Gertrude waited for a crashing sound that didn't come.

Maybe he landed in something soft. She headed toward the closest door and waited.

And waited.

Calvin was the slowest trespasser in the history of trespassing. "Calvin!" she hollered through the door. "Hurry up!"

The door sprang open. "Why must you always be so loud?" he asked as she stepped into the darkness. "What's that?"

"What's what?"

"That giant rope you've got over your shoulder."

"Oh, this is my prepper rope."

"And you've brought it here because you're planning to hang me?"

"Don't be foolish. I brought it here so I could lasso the lamp."

Calvin laughed so hard he began to wheeze. "Oh heavens, you really are trying to kill me."

"What's so funny? What did you think I was going to do? It's not like I'm going to attempt the forklift again. That thing is broken. It only goes in reverse."

"So you're going to grab the lamp with a *rope?*"

"You're the one who's obsessed with westerns!"

"I like to watch them, not try to act them out in a dark thrift store!"

"Oh, come on," she said, pushing past him. Then she said, "No really, come on. I can't see without your headlamp." They walked together then, her leading the way and him providing the light. "There!" she said, pointing upward. "See them? Dead birds!"

Calvin squinted. "Huh. You must have excellent eyesight."

"Indeed, I do. Now step back, this might take me a couple of tries." She began to swing the rope.

He put a hand on hers. "Wait."

"What?"

"Let me try the forklift."

"Why? What makes you think you can drive it?"

"Well, for starters, I'm considerably smarter than you."

Gertrude crossed her arms and waited as Calvin and their only source of light headed toward the forklift. She heard it turn on and then voila! The forklift's headlights came on. Then the forklift headed in her direction.

Well, I'll be darned.

After a few failed attempts, Calvin managed to raise the forks. Up, up, up they went. "Say when," Calvin said. "I can't see too well from in here."

"You couldn't see too well from out here either," Gertrude quipped. "Easy does it! You're almost there! Another few feet!" She was so excited. They had almost done it. "Stop!"

Calvin stopped. He eased the forks under the bin and then, ever so gently, lifted some more. The stack wobbled, but only a little. He backed the forklift up and then lowered the beautiful blue bin to the floor. Gertrude hurried to it and started to grab the lamp.

"Don't touch it!" Calvin cried.

"It's all right!" she said, holding up a hand. "I've got gloves."

Calvin climbed out of the forklift and joined her in gazing down at the world's ugliest dead-bird-lamp. "So, that's it, huh?"

"Yep. And look at this." She pointed at the bottom of the lamp, which had dark, dried blood on it.

Calvin whistled. "Wow, look at that," he said, and pointed to a bloody fingerprint.

"It's the smoking gun," Gertrude said.

16

As they drove north toward Mattawooptock and home, the sun came up, bathing the sky in pinks.

"Well, Gertrude. Looks like we survived the night. But let's not do this again, all right? I'm old. I just want to be retired and bored."

"Really? 'Cause you kind of seemed to be enjoying yourself tonight."

"Yeah, we had an adventure. But what I'm saying is, it was just a one-time thing. I don't want to be your Watson *or* your Sherlock. I just want to sit in my recliner, in my house, and watch my television."

"We'll see," Gertrude said. "Now that we've solved our second case, we could be overwhelmed by paying clients."

"Gertrude, you're not listening. There *is* no we."

"Sure, Calvin. Whatever you say." She didn't believe him for a second.

When they pulled into the trailer park, Gertrude was alarmed to see a cop car parked in her driveway and Hale knocking on her door.

"Do you think he knows?" she asked, her voice shaky with panic.

"I don't know. But does it matter? Aren't you going to tell him anyway, when you give him the lamp?"

"Well, uh, no. I hadn't really gotten that far in my planning," she said thoughtfully. "I was just going to give him the lamp. I wasn't going to tell him where I got it."

Calvin laughed. "Well, sorry, Gert, but I think he's going to ask. Oh, sorry, I know you don't like to be called Gert."

"No, it's all right, Calvin. My friends all call me Gert. All right then, here goes nothing." She climbed out of the car, clutching her prize in one gloved hand. "Hale," she said, nodding. "I have something for you."

Hale turned toward her voice. "Oh yeah?" he said suspiciously.

Calvin climbed out of the car too, and then leaned on it to watch the exchange.

"So, remember the ugly green lamp I told you about before? The murder weapon? Well, I just found it! Someone put it in a bin that was sent to the Goodwill pound store in Gorham. It's got blood all over it. And it's got a bloody fingerprint on it. I'm assuming the blood will match Tislene Breen's and that the print will belong to the murderer. I'll hand it to you if you've got some gloves you can put on."

Hale, apparently speechless, quickly pulled a glove out of his pocket and put it on. Then he reached to pull the lamp from Gertrude's clutches, but she yanked it away.

"Wait," she said firmly.

"What?"

"First, I need to know. Why do you think Roderick did it?"

"What? Why, is that Roderick's print?" Hale asked.

"How should I know? I don't have a fingerprint database in my pocket. But no, since you asked, I am quite certain Roderick did not kill Tislene. But I still want to know why you think he did. And I think I deserve to know, since I just solved the case for you and everything."

Hale's hands dropped to his side.

"You don't *deserve* anything, except maybe handcuffs of your own. Now give me the lamp."

"No," Gertrude put the lamp behind her back.

"Gertrude—" Calvin started, but Hale interrupted.

"You are now obstructing justice," he said.

"Oh fiddlesticks! Just tell me why! I won't tell anyone."

Hale put his hands on his hips and looked around, as if to make sure no one but Calvin was within earshot. Then he leveled an unamused gaze at Gertrude. "A friend of the victim told us that he followed her around. He seemed to have a weird fascination with her. Even followed her out to her car once. So that was enough to search his place, where we found pictures of her." He held out one hand. "Now give me the lamp."

Gertrude thought about it for several seconds and then handed it over. "So you arrested him for being sweet on someone?"

Ignoring her question, he carefully took the lamp from her and gently deposited it in his car.

"He didn't do it," she said.

"OK," Hale said. "But I didn't come here to talk about him. I came to tell you that we caught your burglar."

"Really?" Gertrude asked, surprised.

"Yeah. She looked right at your hidden camera, so it didn't take long to identify her. She's a young woman from Waterville, named Rochelle Price. Do you know her?"

"Don't think so."

"She won't say *why* she broke into your trailer. Something about you buying something from her grandmother, Dawn Price, at a garage sale, something that Miss Price feels should belong to her. But we don't yet know what that something is. She wouldn't say."

Gertrude looked to Calvin for help. He offered none. She turned back to Hale. "How does she know

I'm the one who bought it? It's not like lawnsaleing leaves a paper trail."

Half of Hale's mouth curled up in a smile. "She said that everyone knows you. Apparently, you're a frequent shopper in the area."

"Well, I'll be!" Calvin chirped. "You're a famous lawnsaler. You should call the History channel. Maybe they'll give you your own show!"

Gertrude had no idea what he was talking about, but she was fairly certain it warranted a dirty look. "Pretty sure I'm too young to be on the *History channel*, Calvin." She turned her gaze back to Hale. "Guess I'll have to solve the mystery of the lawn sale burglar later. I am dog-tired."

She started toward her trailer, then thought better of it and turned back to Hale. "You're going to throw the book at her, right?"

Hale smirked. "She has been charged with breaking and entering, yes. But it seems she didn't actually steal anything."

"All right then. Fair enough." She paused, staring at him. Then, "Aren't you going to say thank you?"

"For what?"

"For catching your burglar *and* your murderer?"

He chuckled and looked off into the distance.

Gertrude noticed he was even more handsome in profile.

"This doesn't change anything, you know," he said.

"What?"

He looked at her, with just a hint of his grin remaining. "You're still not a detective. This may or may not even count as evidence in court—"

"I could testify! I'll say I saw it at the murder scene. And I found one of the dead birds then. And then I found the lamp."

"As I was saying, it might not count. There is a process, Gertrude, and you're not part of it. The court will have no way of telling where this lamp really came from or how you really came by it. You shouldn't have jeopardized this case, and you shouldn't have jeopardized your own safety either."

Gertrude looked at Calvin. "Did that sound like a thank you to you, Calvin?" Then she looked at Hale. "Well then, you're welcome, Deputy." And she went inside and closed the door behind her.

Gertrude went straight to bed and slept soundly until three in the afternoon, when a chorus of demanding meows woke her. She had forgotten to give her children breakfast. She poured dry cat food into their bowls and they each gave her a dirty look before delicately digging in. She patted Sleet on the head as he ate, and then realized she was pretty hungry herself. She made herself a tuna fish and pickles sandwich, taking care to drain the tuna can into Sleet's dish. He began to purr.

She balanced her plate on her walker as she made her way into the living room. As she plopped down in her recliner, she realized she was in an unusually good mood. She had really accomplished something. She had helped the police find a murderer, she had cleared Roderick's name, she was sure of it, and she had made a new friend. She smiled as she took a big bite of her sandwich. Then, as she chewed slowly, savoring the crunchy sourness and the creamy mayo, she turned on the tube. Ah, *Antiques Roadshow*. Could this day get any better?

She watched the experts appraise a faded tapestry that turned out to be worth about twenty dollars; a painting that wasn't worth anything; and a Tiffany lamp worth 125,000 dollars. *That* lamp owner burst into tears at the news of her windfall. Gertrude wondered how much the dead-bird-lamp was worth.

The tuna sandwich long gone, Gertrude was just about to drift off to sleep again when the show moved on to an antique salt and pepper shaker set. Gertrude's eyes popped open as she knew she had the same set stashed away. She had picked it up the previous summer at a yard sale for only seventy-five cents.

The little shakers looked like small urns, and if she were to use them, she thought she'd always expect ashes to fall through the small holes.

The appraiser babbled loquaciously until Gertrude was about to throw her shoe at the screen, and then he finally provided a number to justify his excitement: 85,000 dollars.

Gertrude's mouth fell open.

She flew out of the chair, knocking Drizzle off the armrest, flipped on the lights, and furiously dug through her piles until she found her set. Then she hurried back to the television to compare hers to the lottery winner's, but it was too late. They'd moved on to an old rocking chair.

It didn't matter. She was certain. It was the same set.

She called the Somerset County Sheriff's Department and asked to speak to Deputy Hale.

"I'm sorry, ma'am. He's gone home for the evening. Can another deputy help you?"

"Don't call me ma'am, and no, I need to speak to Hale."

"Can I ask what this is regarding?"

"It's a matter of life and death."

"Ma'am, is this an emergency?"

"No. I just need to talk to Hale."

"I'm sorry. That's not possible."

"Look. Just call him. Trust me. He will be glad you did. Tell him to call Gertrude, and tell him it's a matter of *life and death*." She spoke the last few words slowly for emphasis. Then she gave the befuddled woman her phone number. "It's a cellular telephone," Gertrude added. Not because this was pertinent information, but because she was a little proud to own such a thing.

"I'll see what I can do. Are you sure you're not in any danger?"

"Nope."

"And no one else is in any danger?"

"Well I'm sure someone is, somewhere, but I'm the only one in this trailer."

"OK. You have a good night."

Gertrude could hardly stand the waiting. She sat in her chair, but then got back up and paced her narrow paths, never taking her eyes off her phone for more than a few seconds at a time. After a very long ten minutes, Hale called back.

"Hello?" Gertrude said cheerily.

"What?" Hale snapped.

"Did you get the results back on that fingerprint yet?" Gertrude asked.

"No!" Hale barked. "Is that why you interrupted my supper? Dispatch said it was life-or-death!"

"Oh, it absolutely is," Gertrude assured him. "I know what she was after."

"What who was after?"

"The burglar! It was a salt and pepper shaker that I got at a lawn sale in Waterville last summer. It was an awful humid day, but my friend from church took me lawnsaleing. Maybe you know her—her name is Sally? Awful nice lady, though much older than myself. I think that's why she likes spending time with me. I keep her young with all my youthful energy—"

"Please get to the point."

"I've already told you the point! The burglar was after the salt and pepper shaker set, the ugliest things you ever saw, but I guess they're worth a pretty penny. Anyway, you should ask her—"

"I highly doubt she broke into your home, more than once I might add, to steal salt and pepper shakers."

"But she did! I just saw it on *Antiques Roadshow*. One of their hotshot antiquers said it was worth eighty-five grand! And I've got the same set! Mine are in good shape too!"

Hale paused.

"You still there?" she prodded.

"Yes. Well, all right. I'll ask the suspect."

"Thanks. Can you also ask her if she broke in back in September?"

"What? Why?"

"Well someone broke into my trailer back then, but I thought it was the stripper, so I chased her out with a bat."

Hale actually laughed. "A bat, huh? All right. You get some sleep, Gertrude, and please, don't call back." Hale hung up.

So did Gertrude, a broad smile on her face. Nothing felt quite so satisfying as solving a mystery.

17

In the morning, Gertrude knew it was time to go talk to Sherri and resign from her Goodwill position. She had enjoyed working at Goodwill, but she really wanted to devote all her energy to her gumshoe business.

Norman picked her up, and Gertrude regaled him with the whole story, only embellishing a little. In this version, *she* had been the one to dive headfirst through the window, and *she* had been the one to drive the forklift in the desired direction. Norman nodded politely as she talked and looked a little relieved when she disembarked at Goodwill.

When Gertrude found Sherri, her eyes were swollen and red, and black eye makeup ran down her cheeks.

"What's wrong?" Gertrude asked.

"Gertrude, I'm sorry," Sherri said, ignoring her question, "but you don't have a job here anymore. You can't just come and go as you please. It's not fair to the other employees."

"I understand," Gertrude said. "Now, why are you crying?"

Sherri took a deep breath. "Well, the good news is, Roderick has been cleared of all charges. The bad news is, they found the murder weapon, and apparently it had a bloody fingerprint on it."

"And?" Gertrude prodded. So far, none of this was news to her.

"And Azalea has confessed to the murder."

"Azalea?" Gertrude exclaimed. She hadn't seen that one coming. "Why on earth would she kill someone? She's as sweet as cherry pie on Sunday!"

Sherri half-chuckled through fresh tears. "Apparently, Azalea saw the customer hiding items in the cosmetics section. Sometimes people do that when they want to come back and buy them later, when they're half-price. Anyway, Azalea got angry and hit her with a lamp. She says she didn't mean to. She said she just wanted her to stop cheating."

"Hm. That's too bad, Sherri. I know you like Azalea."

Sherri looked at her. "I more than like her. I love her. She's been here with me a long time. She's a sweet girl. You're right, sweet as cherry pie. She really didn't understand what she was doing. I don't think she'd even hurt a fly on purpose. I once saw her pick up a spider in the back room and set it free outside." Gertrude shuddered. "She has a developmental disorder. I know that she did a horrible thing, but I still don't want her to go to *prison*! I just wish none of this had ever happened." Overcome by a new onslaught of tears, Sherri looked at the floor.

"There, there," Gertrude said, and patted her spiky head with one hand. "Don't fret. I think I've got a plan."

Gertrude called Norman back.

"Take me home, Norm, but I only need to be there for a few minutes. Then I need you to take me to the Antiques Mall."

"I hardly think the Antiques Mall is a necessary stop," Norman said.

"It is. Trust me. This is life or death."

"Have you ever heard the story of the boy who cried wolf?"

"Yeah. What about him?"

18

There were two antique stores in Mattawooptock. Both were enormous, and due to some bizarre circumstance Gertrude had yet to figure out, they sat on adjacent properties.

The store to the north was called the Mattawooptock Antiques Mall, and it was a highfalutin, upscale place Gertrude had never stepped foot in.

The store to the south was one of Gertrude's favorite haunts. It was run by a man named Jeff, who didn't talk much but knew everything there was to know about stuff. His store was so full of odds and ends that the walls bulged and the floors sagged. One genuinely had to risk his or her life and limb in order to shop there. The items for sale spilled out of the doors and were stacked atop the roof. Much of his parking lot was taken up by piles of things too large to fit in his stuffed-to-the-gills store.

It was the parking lot of this second store, the one bearing a large, homemade sign that read "Jeff's Junk," that Norman pulled the CAP bus into.

"Not this one," Gertrude snapped. "I said the *Antiques Mall.*"

Norman turned around to look at her. "Seriously?"

"Yes!"

Norman took a deep breath and turned the van around. Gertrude could have just walked the twenty feet between the two parking lots, but several years before, the Antiques Mall had erected a ten-foot tall fence, so that their customers wouldn't have to degrade themselves with the sight of Jeff's Junk.

Finally in the correct parking lot, Gertrude opened the van door. After she climbed out, she said to Norman, "If you wait for me, I'll give you a big tip."

Norman laughed. Gertrude had never tipped him in the three years he'd been driving her around. His laugh suggested that he doubted she had ever tipped anyone at all. Still, he waited.

Gertrude couldn't help sauntering into the Antiques Mall, her treasure safely stowed in her walker pouch. She had even wrapped the shakers in bubble wrap.

She approached the counter, where a slender woman in a black pantsuit stood typing on a computer. Immediately, Gertrude disliked her. Never trust anyone in all black—they obviously don't have cats. Unless of course, they have only black cats. Then they might be all right.

"Can I help you?" the probably-catless woman asked.

"I need to talk to the smartest antique expert you have," Gertrude announced.

"All right. I believe I can help you." The woman smoothed out the front of her jacket as she offered Gertrude a fake smile.

Gertrude leaned in to examine her clothing for cat hairs, and found none. "I also need to talk to the second smartest antique expert you have."

"Just one moment," the woman said. She was still smiling, but her voice came out with a hint of snarl. She picked up a phone and pressed a button. Then she said, "Evan? Could you come to the front please? A customer would like to speak with us."

The woman hung up the phone and stared at Gertrude expectantly. Gertrude stared right back.

"What brings you in today?" the woman tried.

"I'll just wait for Evan," Gertrude said.

Evan eventually appeared. He was wearing a bolo tie and multicolored cowboy boots. This was incredibly strange garb for Mattawooptock, and Evan made Gertrude nervous. She thought about asking to talk to the third smartest expert, but didn't want to press her luck. She also thought about scaling the fence to deal with Jeff, but realized he probably didn't have the kind of cash on hand that she needed.

"*Now* can we help you?" the woman in the pantsuit asked.

"I suppose so." Gertrude reached into her walker pouch and pulled out an old hood ornament, an equally old Zippo, and the salt and pepper shaker urns. She carefully placed them all on the glass countertop. "One of these three things is incredibly valuable. I've come to test your knowledge. Can you tell me which one is worth the most?"

The woman looked exasperated, but Evan looked amused. He looked down at his shorter comrade. "How about it, Miranda? Are you up for a little friendly competition?"

It was clear that Miranda didn't want to play. Evan was growing on Gertrude.

"May I?" he asked Gertrude, motioning to her treasures with one hand.

"Of course."

He picked up the Zippo and looked it over carefully. Then he did the same with the salt shaker. As he flipped it over, he gave a little gasp, which he quickly tried to make up for with a poker face. He failed.

"Are you interested in selling?" he asked, completely abandoning the game.

"For the right price," Gertrude said.

Miranda looked confused. She picked up the salt shaker, looked it over carefully, and then put it back down. Then she looked at Evan, one eyebrow raised. "I don't recognize these. You do?"

"Well," Evan began, "they are old, though not terribly valuable."

"Oh Mylanta!" Gertrude exclaimed. "You're actually lying to her!"

Evan's face flushed. "I most certainly am not!"

Gertrude looked at Miranda. "These are incredibly valuable, and I'll even give you first dibs."

Miranda looked baffled. "I wouldn't know where to begin. I'd have to do some research."

"I'll give you twelve hundred dollars," Evan said.

"Thirteen!" Miranda immediately exclaimed.

Gertrude laughed, and pretended to scoop up her treasures. "Fine. I had a feeling I'd have to go to Bangor to get a real offer anyway."

"Wait," Evan said, putting his hand over Gertrude's, a little more aggressively than she liked. Seeing her expression, he withdrew it. "How much do you want for them?" he asked.

"One hundred thousand dollars!"

Miranda burst into laughter.

"Don't be ridiculous," Evan said.

"And I'll need the money today. Cash or check."

"I'm sorry," Miranda said, "I think you've been misled. There is no way these are worth that much—"

"I'll give you thirty thousand," Evan interrupted.

"Evan!" Miranda exclaimed. "You can't be serious!" Then she looked at Gertrude, "I'll give you thirty-one."

"One hundred thousand," Gertrude repeated, her face stoic.

No one moved or spoke.

Gertrude roughly grabbed the set, intending to shove them back into her walker pouch.

"Careful!" Evan cried, the color draining out of his face.

She slowly removed her hand from the tiny urns.

Evan gulped. "I'll give you 63,000 dollars. It's all I have."

Gertrude looked at Miranda.

She just stood there with her mouth hanging open.

Gertrude extended her right hand across the counter, with pomp.

Tentatively, Evan took it in his own.

"You've got a deal," Gertrude said, and smiled.

Gertrude climbed back into the van, exhausted.

"Where's my tip?" Norman asked.

"I need to cash this check first."

"Really? You actually got money?"

"Yes, please take me to the credit union."

"Which one?"

"Don't care. Then I need to go to the Law Offices of Hibbard and Mead."

"Lawyers? What have you done, Gertrude?"

"It's not for me, Norm. Let's go. Time's a wastin'."

"I know, I know, it's life or death," he said, and put the van in drive.

Gertrude marched into the fancy law office and up to the gaudy welcome desk with confidence.

"May I help you?" a well-dressed woman asked.

"Yes. I need to talk to the best criminal lawyer you have."

"Very well. Do you have an appointment?"

"No. But I do have a lot of money in my satchel."

The woman looked amused. "All right. If you will just have a seat in the waiting area, I'll find someone who can speak with you."

Gertrude sat down in a leather wing chair, which she figured cost more than her trailer, and almost fell asleep. But soon she heard a man's voice say, "I'm Charlie Hibbard. Can I help you?"

She looked up at him. He was tall, dark, and handsome. He was clean shaven and wearing a tie. "Are you a lawyer?"

"Yes, ma'am."

"Are you a good one?"

"I believe I am, yes."

"Good. Because I need to hire you to defend my friend Azalea. I sold some ugly urn shakers so I could pay you. She killed someone, but she's a nice girl. So you've got to keep her out of prison."

"My retainer is twenty-five thousand dollars," he said doubtfully.

"That would be fine."

"All right then, won't you step into my office?"

Norman dropped Gertrude back off at Goodwill. She found Sherri in the back, her eyes still raccooned with smeared mascara.

"It's going to be right as rain," Gertrude told her.

Sherri looked at her questioningly.

"I've just hired Charlie Hibbard to represent Azalea. I gave him the facts of the case, and he said he could help. He was actually quite full of himself, which I suppose, in this case, is a good thing. Anyway, he said that he would help Azalea go to a nice place, where people can help her. He said the trial would be a piece of cake."

"No prison?" Sherri said hopefully.

"No prison. He practically promised it. When I left, he was calling the district attorney, who is an old college buddy of his. I guess they were in the same fraternity or something. They still play golf together. Though not right now. On account of it being December and all."

Sherri stood there, open-mouthed and wide-eyed.

Gertrude waited for her to say something.

Finally, she said, "Are you sure?"

"Am I sure? Of course I'm sure! I just left there!"

"But Gertrude, how could you ever afford to hire a lawyer?"

"Oh that. Well, I just sold some tiny urns at the Antiques Mall."

Sherri burst into laughter at that. It was a disconcerting, out-of-control cackle that made her look, not to mention sound, a little unhinged. Gertrude took a step back.

"For real?" Sherri cried, still laughing. "This is real? Azalea won't go to prison?"

"I just said that."

"Oh, Gertrude!" Sherri cried and bear-hugged her.

"Sherri!" Gertrude squeaked. "You're squeezing me really tight!"

Sherri let go and held her out at arm's length. "Oh, sorry." She laughed maniacally again. "Gertrude! I take it back! You can work here! You can have as many hours as you like! You're a hero!" She bear-hugged her again.

Gertrude had a thought. "I don't really want to work here, Sherri. I was just doing it to catch a killer. But I'll tell you what you *can* do for me."

"What?" Sherri said, still hugging her.

"Can you let me go through the Gorham bins before the truck comes to pick them up? I've been banned from the pound store."

Sherri stepped back and smiled. "Absolutely, Gertrude. I think that sounds like a fine idea."

87040877R00087

Made in the USA
Columbia, SC
08 January 2018